When they reached her door, she turned around to look at him.

Emotions were escalating within her. Longing was beginning to be a familiar companion. "Would you like to come in?" she asked him.

"No. If I come in, that practically guarantees that you won't go to bed for at least another half hour, if not longer. I don't want to be responsible for having you wind up dragging all day tomorrow," he told her, even though the words cost him. "We'll just say good-night right here."

She thought Wyatt meant just that. That he would leave her right here with only his parting words echoing in his wake.

Rachel didn't want to throw herself at him, but she didn't want the evening to end this way, either.

And while she was thinking about this, debating what move she could make, she suddenly felt his hands framing her face.

The next moment, he brought his own down to it.

Her heart began to hammer the moment Wyatt's lips touched hers.

* * *

MATCHMAKING MAMAS

Dear Reader,

Everyone would rather forget the year 2020. However, one really good thing happened three days into the year. My long-awaited grandson, Logan, finally made his first appearance. All five pounds of him. That made everything else a little more bearable for my family.

Since we all need something to distract us, this is my offering to you. Another Matchmaking Mamas story, in which a father's slow recovery from an almost debilitating heart attack put his daughter's whole life on hold while she took care of him as well as ran the family business. Feeling terribly guilty because his daughter's fiancé abandoned her and went on to marry someone else, George Fenelli is desperate to make things up to his daughter now. To him, that means finding someone who's worthy of his daughter. To that end, he goes to see Maizie Sommers, an old friend and one of the three Matchmaking Mamas. Things take off from there.

I wrote this book while I was recovering from some pretty heavy-duty foot surgery. I was relegated off my feet and confined to a walker (and home) for three months. Since my normal speed is ninety miles an hour, this was really rough. In addition, during the last week of October, wildfires came within miles of our house. We were on standby to evacuate. Consequently, writing was not always as easy as it normally is for me. Bearing this in mind, I really hope you enjoy reading this.

As always, from the bottom of my heart, I wish you someone to love who loves you back and offer up my fervent hope that 2021 has been far better for all of us than the previous year was.

With love,

Marie Ferrarella

The Late Bloomer's Road to Love

MARIE FERRARELLA

Recycling programs for this product may not exist in your area.

ISBN-13: 978-1-335-40804-4

The Late Bloomer's Road to Love

This edition published by arrangement with Harlequin Books S.A.

For questions and comments about the quality of this book, please contact us at CustomerService@Harlequin.com.

Harlequin Enterprises ULC
22 Adelaide St. West, 40th Floor
Toronto, Ontario M5H 4E3, Canada
www.Harlequin.com

Printed in U.S.A.

USA TODAY bestselling and RITA® Award–winning author **Marie Ferrarella** has written more than three hundred books for Harlequin, some under the name Marie Nicole. Her romances are beloved by fans worldwide. Visit her website, marieferrarella.com.

Books by Marie Ferrarella

Harlequin Special Edition

Matchmaking Mamas

Coming Home for Christmas
Dr. Forget-Me-Not
Twice a Hero, Always Her Man
Meant to Be Mine
A Second Chance for the Single Dad
Christmastime Courtship
Engagement for Two
Adding Up to Family
Bridesmaid for Hire
Coming to a Crossroads
The Late Bloomer's Road to Love

Visit the Author Profile page
at Harlequin.com for more titles.

To

Logie Bear

On His First Birthday.

Time Really Flies By Fast.

You'll Be Asking To Borrow

The Car Before I Know It.

All My Love,

G-Mama

Prologue

George Fenelli looked quite good for a man who'd had an all but debilitating heart attack almost two years ago. A born fighter, George had come back from that the way he had from all the curveballs, large and small, that life had thrown him.

What he wasn't able to overcome was his discomfort for the reason why he was sitting across from Maizie Sommers in her real estate office. He had known Maizie a long time. Known her long before his beloved Marilyn had died, leaving him to soldier on and raise their only daughter,

Rachel, on his own. His friendship with Maizie went way back.

As a matter of fact, it was Maizie who had sold him the restaurant that he had worked hard to build up and had turned into the thriving, trendy go-to eatery it had become. From the very beginning, working at the restaurant had been a labor of love for George, his wife and daughter, even though Marilyn had a full-time job as a nurse and Rachel had been a middle school student. Whenever they could spare the time, they worked at the restaurant. He had to admit that it was Marilyn's salary that had kept them afloat those days, when money had been tight.

Gradually, things changed and the restaurant had become a success. It was around that time that Marilyn began to grow ill. Three years later, she was gone and the restaurant was the only thing that kept George going. He pushed on relentlessly, doing the work of three men.

And that was the problem. Just when Rachel graduated high school—with honors—and was about to go off to college with the young man she considered to be the love of her life, George had suffered a heart attack.

Rachel never hesitated for a moment. She immediately put a halt to all her plans. Despite his protests, she remained by his side through the surgeries and then his slow, long road back to the land of the living. Somehow, with her relentless determination, she also continued to run the restaurant that she knew like the back of her hand. What that meant was that she slept in snatches and worked like a demon the rest of the time.

Meanwhile, she had to forfeit over two years of her life, as well as the man with whom she had thought she was going to share the rest of her life.

George was determined to make it up to her, to give Rachel back at least part of what she had lost because of him. Which was ultimately what had brought him to Maizie's office.

"Don't get me wrong, I'm not talking about her getting back together with that fickle creep, Elliott James," he told Maizie. "If you ask me, my girl is better off without him."

"You're talking about her former fiancé, right?" Maizie asked.

How Maizie kept everyone's life straight in her head was beyond George, but that was why he had sought her out to begin with. She was exceedingly bright and intuitive and he needed her to apply her special magic to Rachel's life.

Word had gotten around that Maizie and her two lifelong best friends, Theresa and Cilia, dabbled in matchmaking on the side, although all of them ran their own businesses, as well. So far, there hadn't been a mismatch among all the people they'd helped—and George's hopes had soared when he'd heard that.

A man worthy of his daughter—that was what he was looking for.

Someone far different from her disgusting ex. "Yes, the one who thought nothing of leaving her behind the moment he found someone else to tickle his fancy, or whatever they call it these days," he said. "That loser's married now, you know."

"Yes, so I've heard," Maizie answered. "I take it that despite your recovery, Rachel hasn't gone back to college yet?"

He shook his head. "She won't hear of it. She's afraid if she leaves me, I'll start to overdo it again and have another heart attack. You ask me, Rachel's the candidate for a heart attack. She's running the restaurant *and* taking courses online at night. Don't ask me when she sleeps. I don't think she does."

Maizie did her best to get the facts straight. "I thought you were back at the restaurant."

He sighed. Life had certainly gotten out of kilter. "I am, but only part-time. Rachel refuses to hear about me going back full-time until I complete the physical therapy requirements the doctor insisted on. Rachel's the one who's running Vesuvius." He frowned, thinking about the physical therapists he had been saddled with. "The therapists I've tried so far I haven't liked, but Rachel won't let me give up. She's determined to have her way. She's stubborn, like her mother," he added with a faint smile.

"Uh-huh." *More like her father,* Maizie thought, although she kept that to herself.

Normally, Maizie was an exceedingly patient woman, but she had clients coming in shortly, so she tried to coax George along a little, although she was certain she knew exactly where this was heading.

Matchmaking.

Matchmaking had just started out as something she and her friends had undertaken to nudge their children in the right direction when it came to finding someone to share their lives with.

When that had turned out so well, they'd just decided to continue. There was an unspoken agreement among them that if any of the matches they made wound up failing, they would cease their efforts. But so far, they still hadn't failed. Every couple they brought together had gotten married and remained together.

Every single one of them.

It was a track record all three were exceedingly proud of.

Maizie decided it was time to prod George along just a little. "Everything going well at the restaurant?"

"Absolutely. We have more business than we can handle," he told her.

"Wonderful," she replied with enthusiasm, her mouth curving. "And you're not in the market for a new house, are you?"

This time his response was more emphatic. "Oh, no, that's the house where Rachel was born, where Marilyn and I made all those wonderful memories. I have no intention of *ever* selling it."

Maizie nodded. She could understand that. "Then I take it you're here because of my other 'vocation.' And since I'm assuming that you're not looking for a date at this stage of your life, I take it this is about a match for Rachel." As she said the words, she saw George cringe. "Something wrong?"

"No, it just sounds so businesslike, not to mention that it seems like I'm pushing my nose where it doesn't belong." He was painfully aware of what Rachel would say if she ever found out what he was doing.

Maizie smiled. "Ah, the business of romance is a very important part of our lives, George.

There's nothing wrong with that. Sometimes strings have to be pulled. I just need to make certain that that *is* your intent. And don't worry, unless you tell her yourself, Rachel is never going to find out that any of this was arranged. I promise," she added very seriously.

Rather than say yes, he told her, "Because of me, Rachel put going to college on hold. And because of that, she stayed behind while her worthless fiancé went to college."

"If his attention span is that short, George, maybe he's not such a loss," Maizie said.

"Oh, I know he's not," George agreed. "Rachel deserves someone who's worthy of her." He smiled at Maizie. "I'd really like for you and your friends to make that happen."

"Well, I'll certainly see what we can do," Maizie promised.

He rose to his feet, nodding at the woman. "That's all I ask, Maizie, that's all I ask," he told her very seriously. "Let me know what I can do. And spare no expense. Whatever it comes to, I'll cover. That girl is everything to me. She always has been."

"There's no cost, George, just ingenuity." Hooking her arm through his, Maizie walked the man to the front door. "And I understand what you're saying, George. Believe me, I totally understand," she told him, sympathetically, patting his arm. "I'll be in touch," she promised.

He knew that when Maizie said it, she meant it. It was just a matter of time.

He left the real estate office feeling happier and more hopeful than he had been in a long time.

Rachel was as good as married, he thought. This time to a decent man.

He knew that he could bet his life on that.

"Our girl's in good hands, Marilyn," he whispered under his breath as he got into his car to drive back to the restaurant.

Chapter One

"Okay, Maizie, we came as fast as we could without breaking any of the speed limits," Cilia Parnell announced as she walked in through the front door of her friend's cozy, two-story house. She was closely followed by Theresa Manetti, the third member of what Maizie liked to, on occasion, refer to as the dynamic trio. "So what's the big emergency?"

"No big emergency, ladies. Just some good news," Maizie told her two oldest, closest friends, women she had known since third grade, as she shut the front door behind them.

Bedford was an exceedingly peaceful city,

deemed to be one of the safest cities of its size in the country for more than twenty-five years running, but Maizie still automatically closed the door and locked it. To her way of thinking, there was no reason to tempt fate. So she didn't.

"All right," Cilia said gamely. "Then what's the 'good news'?"

Maizie led her friends into the family room, which more often than not doubled as the game room where they played poker. The table was cleared and appeared set for a new game to begin. The cards were stacked on one side and there were chips—the crunchy kind—on the opposite side, ready to be consumed during the course of a game.

Cilia and Theresa took it all in, and as they did, their smiles grew decidedly wider. They rarely played just for fun. They played, instead, to discuss strategy.

Theresa turned toward Maizie. "We have a romance to kindle, don't we?" she cried, delighted.

It had been a while since they had gotten their last couple together and she, like the other two, missed the thrill that matchmaking always generated for them.

Theresa, even more than the others, was a hopeless romantic.

Maizie inclined her head. There was no point

in stretching this out. "Yes, ladies, we have a romance to kindle," she echoed. And then her mouth curved in amusement. "Unless, of course, you two have something better to do."

"You're kidding, right?" Theresa asked incredulously. "Every single dinner I cater, every single cake I bake, all I do is dream of the next time we can bring a couple who have no idea that they were meant to be together—together," she concluded with a deep, contented sigh, her eyes shining in anticipation.

"And even though house cleaning doesn't usually enter into the romance picture," Cilia declared loftily, referring to the business she had started on a whim and built up into the thriving enterprise it had now become, "it doesn't stop me from dreaming about it being a means to an end, same as you."

Theresa looked at Cilia, puzzled. "What?"

"Never mind, I know what I mean," Cilia said with a wave of her hand. She made herself comfortable at the card table, although actually playing cards was the farthest thing from her mind—or any of their minds—right now. "All right, Maizie, stop being so coy. Out with it. Details," she cried. "We need details."

If anyone was keeping score, it was Maizie, who usually brought in at least fifty percent of the matches they had worked on. The candidates were brought to her by friends, or friends of friends who had heard about the successful efforts of the trio. In essence these people came asking for help in finding soul mates for their children or relatives who had become so absorbed in work that the hope of finding someone didn't exist. Or, had been so disappointed by someone they thought had cared about them that they'd vowed never to go that painful route again.

From their very first successful undertaking, Maizie, Theresa and Cilia had become hooked on matchmaking. They'd silently decided that it was up to the three of them to sift through the people they were helping until they could bring together the perfect match.

Maizie knew that made the situation sound far more complicated than it actually was, but she didn't try to explain it to anyone anymore. She and her friends just forged ahead and did whatever they felt was necessary to "make the magic happen," as she had once described the process to her daughter, several years after she and her friends had united her daughter with the widower who was destined to become her husband.

Everyone, Maizie maintained, loved love.

Cilia now looked at the woman she and Theresa had always thought of as "the ringleader" of their small band, especially as they were years younger.

"You know, you're being awfully secretive about this, Maizie," she said.

Maizie smiled broadly. "It's not *secretive*, dear. It's called savoring the moment."

Cilia pressed her lips together. "Well, I don't know what you call it, but I call it being annoying."

For once, Theresa, usually the very patient, easygoing one of the trio, was not living up to her reputation.

"Enough with the banter, you two," she told her friends, then gave Maizie a sharp, penetrating look. "Talk!"

Surprised and amused, Cilia laughed under her breath as she leaned in toward Theresa. "First time she had to be told to do that."

Both sets of expectant eyes turned toward Maizie.

"Well?" Cilia asked after a beat, her eyes all but boring into the real estate agent's face. "Just how long are you planning on drawing this out, oh fearless leader?"

"Sorry," Maizie apologized, still very amused by her friends' reactions. "You'll forgive me, but it has been a long time since our last 'challenge.'"

"And you doing this is definitely making the experience a lot longer," Cilia pointed out, her voice growing somewhat short with her friend. All three women would have gladly given up their lives for one another, but their time was a slightly different matter. They were busier now than they had been years ago. No one cared about the lure of retirement.

Maizie laughed softly. "All right, all right, the wait is over, ladies." And with that, she launched into the details as they had been laid out for her by George Fenelli.

When Maizie had concluded her short summation, she had a pertinent question for Theresa. If she remembered correctly, this would go right to the heart of the matter and make things easy for them.

"Theresa, didn't you once tell me that you had a cousin whose son had become a physical therapist?"

It took Theresa a moment to recall who Maizie was referring to. And then she frowned slightly. "Oh, you mean my cousin Ariel." Theresa was a very kindhearted woman, but it was obvious that cousin or not, Ariel was not her favorite person. "Yes. Ariel was very disappointed that Wyatt chose to become a physical therapist instead of an orthopedic surgeon, or at least *some* sort of a doctor. Every time I run into her at family gatherings, it takes her less than five minutes before she starts to complain that she doesn't know why her younger son decided to waste his life this way and didn't become a doctor."

"Sounds to me as if what this Ariel is really focused on is having some sort of bragging rights that reflect well on her," Cilia speculated.

Theresa nodded, barely looking at the cards that Maizie had dealt her. "You've certainly got that right," she agreed. Her expression softened with sympathy. "And Wyatt is really such a great guy. He has this way about him that just brings out the best in people." She shook her head as her eyes met Maizie's. "You know, I never understood why that boy is still single." She bit her lower lip as she said, "Maybe it's because Ariel winds up intimidating any young woman who Wyatt brings home and introduces her to."

Maizie nodded. She was familiar with the type. The woman probably thought that no one was good enough for her son.

"So this might be a double challenge," she speculated.

For a moment, Theresa had been lost in thought. But hearing Maizie's comment had her mind coming front and center. Her eyes suddenly lit up as she looked at Maizie. "Are you thinking of matching up Wyatt with...?"

The young man was single and had the necessary profession they were looking for. Those were definitely the first two qualifications.

"Why not?" Maizie responded with her all-but-disarming smile.

"Why not indeed," Cilia murmured under her breath, nodding.

"Do you happen to have a picture of the young man?" Maizie asked. It wouldn't hurt to know just what he looked like. Looks weren't everything, but heaven knew they didn't hurt.

"He's family, Maizie. Of course I have a picture," Theresa responded, taking out her cell phone. "It'll just take me a few minutes to locate a recent one, that's all."

Maizie laughed, rising from the card table. "I know what that means. I'll go get us something to drink."

Theresa had managed to successfully flip through her photos by the time Maizie returned from the kitchen with the tray of beverages.

"Here he is," Theresa declared, holding up her cell phone for the others to see. "Wyatt Watson."

Setting the tray down, Maizie nodded her approval. And then she took the cell phone from Theresa in order to get a closer look. "That boy is definitely cute," she pronounced. "And he's not spoken for?" She handed the phone back to Theresa.

"Not even so much as a whisper," Theresa replied. "He's been very busy, first going to classes and then putting all that knowledge to work, taking twice as many clients as the other therapists. From what I gather, Wyatt is a regular whirlwind and exceptionally dedicated. I hear that he formed his own company recently."

"Ambitious," Maizie nodded. "That definitely sounds good," she said, half to herself. Her eyes swept over her friends as she leaned back in her chair. "Well, I'd say that from the looks of it, we have ourselves a perfect candidate for a good match."

"Do we have any idea what the other half of this 'good match' looks like?" Theresa asked.

"As a matter of fact, we do. Rachel Fenelli—" it occurred to Maizie that she had not used the young woman's full name yet "—runs the family restaurant while taking college courses at night. The girl never sleeps," she said, repeating what George had told her. "She wants to be a nurse just like her late mother."

Cilia nodded her head at the information. "Perfect. If this works, they can get married and set up their own clinic."

Maizie knew that Cilia was just kidding, but she gave the matter some thought. "You know, that isn't a half-bad idea."

"That's because I don't have any bad ideas," Cilia told her friend. She was only half kidding.

Maizie gave her friend a patient smile. "This is not the time to let your ego take over," she told Cilia. And then she clapped her hands together. This had been a very productive meeting. "Well, ladies, I think we call Rachel's father and tell him that we believe we have the perfect solution for his problem and just possibly the perfect man for his daughter."

"Wait, he has a problem?" Theresa asked, concerned. "What sort of a problem?"

"It seems that part of his deal with Rachel was that she would allow him to come back to work at the restaurant if he went to see a physical therapist the way his doctor suggested," Maizie told her friends. "So far, according to him, he's rejected every therapist that the agency sent to him."

"Why?" Cilia asked.

"It's kind of like 'Goldilocks and the Three Bears.' You know, each therapist was either too pushy, too laid-back or too something. But I have a feeling that Wyatt is going to be just right. I'll have a talk with George to make sure of that," she promised the two women. Looking at them, she paused for a moment, then asked, "So, what do you say? Shall we get started on this?"

"You don't have to twist my arm," Cilia said. "Theresa?" she asked, looking at the third member of the group.

"I'll give Wyatt a call and let him know that I need his expertise to help a dear friend of mine get some much-needed physical therapy," Theresa said, smiling at the idea.

Maizie nodded. "Sounds like a plan." And then she smiled broadly. "Well, that certainly didn't take us long." She looked from one friend to the other. "What do you say that we actually play a game of poker for old times' sake?"

Cilia laughed. "Okay. I think I still actually remember how."

Theresa exchanged looks with Maizie. Neither were taken in for a moment. "You know what that means," Theresa told the latter.

"Hold on to your money," Maizie said with a laugh.

Pleasure highlighted Cilia's expression. "You know I really have missed this."

"What? Losing to me?" Maizie asked, her mouth curving.

"Maizie, you didn't tell me your memory's been slipping," Cilia deadpanned.

"That's because it hasn't been," she responded. Her hands flew as she shuffled and dealt the cards in earnest. "Prepare to be separated from your money."

It was a lofty statement considering that their high-stakes game usually involved pennies and the biggest haul any of them ever made came to a grand total of five dollars, all in change.

As the game progressed—and they made plans as to how to unobtrusively get the two young people together—Maizie smiled to herself. She dearly loved getting her real estate clients into the home of their dreams, but she had to admit that there was no greater satisfaction than bringing two people together. Every single couple they had united had eventually gotten married and gone on to start families of their own.

Counting their own children, that made a grand total of twenty-eight couples.

Not exactly an overwhelming number of people when all things were considered, but each couple was exceedingly happy, and as far as Maizie was concerned, this was their small contribution to the peace and happiness of their current orderly little world.

"What are you grinning about?" Cilia asked. "You're not cheating, are you?" she deadpanned, knowing full well that neither she nor her two friends would ever even remotely consider cheating. There was no fun in winning that way.

“No, I’m not cheating. I’m anticipating,” Maizie answered.

“Anticipating?” Theresa echoed. “Anticipating what?”

“Anticipating how happy Wyatt and Rachel are about to become—and they haven’t got the slightest idea what’s out there, just waiting to slip into their lives and surround them,” Maizie answered.

“They might not have any idea,” Cilia agreed, her smile widening. “But we certainly do.”

Theresa winked at her lifelong friends. “Yes, we certainly do,” she agreed. “Deal faster, Cilia.”

“Yes, ma’am,” Cilia responded. “When did she get so bossy? I don’t remember her being this bossy, but then, we haven’t been getting together that much lately.”

“Haven’t you noticed? She’s always been that way.” Maizie looked at Theresa. “It’s the quiet ones you have to watch out for.”

There was no arguing that.

Chapter Two

Her neck was killing her.

She'd done it again, Rachel thought with a weary sigh, straightening up in her chair as she rubbed the back of her neck.

Every bone in her body was protesting.

Loudly.

Despite the promise she had made to herself—over and over again—she had fallen asleep at her computer.

Again.

Served her right, she supposed with another deep sigh. She'd put in what felt like a day and a half at the restaurant yesterday, and then, after coming home, instead of crawling into bed the way every bone in her body begged her to, she had opened up her computer and turned it on "just for a minute."

She had promised herself she'd merely "look" at something in the class notes she had taken and then that would be the end of it.

Except that it wasn't.

Because that had led to just "peeking into" the ongoing class that was in session and that—well, that had ultimately resulted in her using the keyboard for what turned out to be an extremely uncomfortable pillow.

The sad thing was that it wasn't the first time.

Rachel sighed and stretched, doing her best to realign her neck and spine. There was no point in upbraiding herself. Besides, she didn't have time for that, anyway.

Glancing at her watch as she padded into the bathroom, she realized that she had about an hour to shower, get dressed and get to the restaurant. It was time to prepare for another day—and the Rafferty celebration. If she didn't get moving, she was going to slip off the treadmill she was on and then suddenly she would find herself even more behind than she usually was. Not a good thing.

Rachel took one of her trademark five-minute

showers—and that included getting dressed and drying her hair. She was on the stairs, making her way down into the kitchen in what was an absurdly small amount of time. Her mind was doing its best to catch up.

The tempting smell of bacon and eggs met her before her foot had a chance to even hit the bottom of the stairs.

It looked as if her father was up ahead of her—again. She had to admit that she had missed that aroma those long, long months when he had been recuperating. But while she was happy he was trying to get back to his old self, she was worried that he was rushing the process and it could very possibly take its toll on him.

She didn't want to think about the consequences of that. It was bad enough losing her mother years ago. The idea of losing her father was too awful to even contemplate.

Walking into the kitchen, Rachel saw that her father was fully dressed and at the stove.

He had the timing down pat. Breakfast was ready and on two plates by the time she crossed the threshold.

Her father looked as good as ever. Maybe a little too energetic, she thought, taking a closer look at the man. Was he trying to throw her off?

"Smells good, Dad." She took her place at

the table, sitting down. "Looks good, too." Any offer she made to help him would be rejected and might even offend his self-esteem. This was definitely a tightrope she walked every day. "As do you," she added. "Maybe a little too good."

"Thank you," George said. "I think a man can never look too good."

Raising her eyes to his face, she said pointedly, "He can if all he's supposed to do is hang around the house and take it easy."

"Ah, well, we might have a problem there," George answered as he took a seat at the small kitchen table directly opposite Rachel.

Instantly alert, Rachel raised her eyebrows. "Dad, you're not planning on doing what I think you're planning on doing, are you?" she asked sharply, although she felt she already knew the answer.

"That all depends," he said innocently, avoiding Rachel's eyes. "What is it that you think I'm planning on doing?"

"Dad." There was a warning note in her voice.

George sighed. This was no time to be playing games. "All right, for the record, I'm planning on going into *my* restaurant today. All day if a certain killjoy doesn't have her way."

"Dad, we talked about this," Rachel reminded him, trying not to lose her patience.

She understood what he was undoubtedly feeling, but she didn't want him taking unnecessary chances. He still hadn't complied with the doctor's instructions to avail himself of physical therapy. So far, he had dismissed every therapist who had shown up, for one reason or another. She had a sneaking suspicion that her father wasn't nearly as recovered as he was trying to make her believe.

"Endlessly, as I remember," George replied wearily.

Rachel pressed her lips together. She respected him, but her father was behaving just like a little boy. He was constantly looking for a way around the problem, creating another one.

"And what conclusion did we come to?" Rachel asked expectantly.

George flashed his daughter a tolerant smile. "Well, if you can't remember, maybe you're the one who has been working way too hard."

Rachel gritted her teeth together. "The conclusion we came to was that until you have those physical therapy sessions that the doctor wants you to have, you're not going to go back to the restaurant—unless it's to grab a bite to eat or just say hi to the staff," she said pointedly. He had already snuck in a few times, trying to take his rightful place back at the restaurant. At an age where some men were longing for retirement, her father insisted on working harder than ever.

"I've had physical therapy sessions," George informed her.

Rachel humored her father. "Yes, you have," she agreed. "And you've fired every single one of the therapists. A record number of eight therapists as I recall." She saw her father opening his mouth to protest and she cut him off. "You know, until this whole thing happened, I would have said you were a very easygoing guy."

"I *am* an easygoing guy," George insisted, finishing his breakfast.

"That is *not* what all those therapists you fired would say."

He frowned. He would have thought that Rachel, of all people, would have understood what the problem was. She might look like her mother, but she took after him. "I had a heart attack, Rachel, but there's nothing wrong with my brain. I refuse to be treated like a doddering old fool," he told her heatedly, thinking of his interaction with some of the therapists.

"You're not a doddering old fool, Dad." Rachel sighed. "Maybe you're taking offense where none was intended."

"I'm not imagining things, Rachel," he told

her, trying to keep his temper. He knew she meant well, but she hadn't been in his shoes.

"I didn't say that," she protested. Finished with breakfast, she rose from the table. "Tell you what, I'll try to stick around for the next therapist—provided you're going to get another one. Otherwise, all bets are off, and your doctor will back me up."

George sighed a little too deeply, since he knew—but couldn't let on—about the plan that was in place. "I suppose I have to if I ever want to get back to working for more than a few minutes at a time."

She hadn't realized what a drama queen her father could be. "I've let you stay on for more than a few minutes at a time, Dad," she reminded him.

He sighed. He missed the hustle of the restaurant, the challenges. "Distributing napkins from a seated position is not my idea of 'staying on.'"

"Take it or leave it, Dad." She gathered her purse and notes together.

George shook his head, looking at his only offspring sadly. "You know, you're getting more and more like your mother every day."

She knew that underneath it all, he meant that as a compliment. Rachel smiled at her father broadly. "You know I'm right."

"That's beside the point," he said dismissively. "And for your information, a new therapist is coming over today. So why don't I accompany you to *my* restaurant and then later, you can meet and grill my new therapist. Is it a deal?"

She eyed him skeptically. Her father had conveniently "forgotten" things before, or gotten things confused. "There's really a therapist coming this afternoon?"

"Yes," he answered tolerantly. "There's really a therapist coming this afternoon."

"What's her name?" Rachel asked, thinking that her father was just paying lip service to the whole situation. This so-called therapist could conveniently be a no-show, or forget to come.

"The therapist's name is Wyatt Watson," George answered with a smile, pleased with himself that he recalled the name that Maizie had told him.

Rachel looked at her father in surprise. Up until now, all the therapists her father had seen—and dismissed—had been women.

"The therapist is a man?" she questioned.

George recalled the words that Maizie had told him. She had suggested that they might be helpful in winning his daughter over. "The agency thought I'd have more luck with a man."

Rachel thought of all the therapists her father

had found fault with for one reason or another. "You know, they might have a point."

"So, is it a deal? Can I come to the restaurant?" he asked eagerly.

It almost broke her heart. But she knew she had to stay strong for his sake. She was doing this for her father's own good, not because she wanted to control him.

"What time is the therapist coming?" she asked.

"He'll be here before noon," he told her.

She hadn't thought the therapist would be coming so soon. She wouldn't get a chance to meet and observe this latest candidate. "All right, then you can come to the restaurant this afternoon, after your session. Just make sure you bring a note from this Wyatt person."

"You are definitely a hard woman to bargain with," George said to his daughter.

Rachel acknowledged his comment with a smile. "Yes, I know. Now I've got to get to the restaurant to get ready for the lunch crowd," she said, walking away from the table.

"I could help," her father offered.

She turned around and gave him a look. "You can help by seeing your new therapist—and not terminating him in the first twenty minutes."

"How about the first half hour?" George deadpanned.

Part of her felt he wasn't kidding. "Dad," she said in a warning voice.

George raised his hands as if fending off an overzealous puppy. "I'm kidding, I'm kidding," he told her. And then he became serious. "I've got a good feeling about this one."

Rachel allowed a tired sigh to escape. "Well, I certainly hope so," she said. "Because I have no intentions of letting you wiggle out of this. You are going to see a therapist and listen to whatever he has to say, then follow up with the exercises he wants you to do."

"Yes, ma'am." He said it so solemnly that Rachel almost believed him.

Or maybe she just wanted to.

She paused by the front door to issue a warning.

"I'm holding you to that."

"I wouldn't expect anything less," George assured his daughter.

Flashing him a smile, Rachel lost no time in flying out the front door.

"You know, this has to be a first, Aunt Theresa," Wyatt told the woman who was technically his mother's cousin and not her sibling.

But somehow, it just didn't seem right calling her "cousin." Especially not since she was a good twenty-five years older than he was. "I have to admit, it feels rather nice not to have to deal with that disappointed look that always slips over my mother's face every time she has an occasion to 'discuss' my chosen profession."

Theresa laughed. "Your mother grew up watching a lot of doctor programs. I think she had a crush on one or two of the main actors in some of the series." She smiled, pausing and patting his hand. "I'm sure that she's very proud of the therapist you've become."

"Well, that makes one of us because if she is, she's kept it a big secret," Wyatt confessed. He saw that the woman was about to protest his assessment. "That's okay, Aunt Theresa, I get my satisfaction from helping my clients."

Theresa was moving around the kitchen of her catering business, checking on various things. Wyatt followed her around, keeping a respectful distance. "Speaking of which, how did you happen to get this man's name you're asking me to see?"

Theresa flashed him a smile, not wanting to get into it. When she lied, she had a tendency to slip up. "It's a long story, dear," she said, checking on the cake that was in the oven. "He's one of

Maizie's friends and when I heard that he was in need of a good physical therapist, I immediately thought of you. I hope you don't mind."

Theresa was confident that Wyatt wouldn't turn her down. Ever since he had been a small boy, he had always been all about helping people. He had a heart as big as all outdoors.

"Mind? I don't know if you know this or not, but I've started up my own company recently. That's always been my ultimate goal," Wyatt explained.

She smiled warmly at him. She couldn't understand why her cousin Ariel wasn't proud of this hardworking son of hers. "Sounds ambitious."

"Practical, actually," he clarified. "Having someone standing and looking over my shoulder was good when I was learning my way around all this, but once I grew more confident—once I knew what I was doing—having someone second-guessing me and redirecting what I was doing just undermined my clients' confidence in me. No conceit intended, but I knew that I was doing the right thing. Being monitored by a 'superior' interfered with the way I was connecting with my clients," he said as he continued to follow her around the kitchen area. Wyatt had to admit that the aroma was getting to him, whetting his taste buds.

Theresa nodded. “You were right, of course. Practical,” she pronounced. She took out a folded piece of paper from her pocket and handed the paper to Wyatt. “This is the address. I was hoping that you might be able to get started right away.”

“What's the hurry?” Wyatt asked, glancing at the address. He was familiar with the area. “Is this George Fenelli having a lot of difficulties functioning?”

Theresa glanced at him over her shoulder. “Actually,” she admitted, “this has more to do with his daughter.”

Wyatt frowned slightly. “I don't think I understand.”

“Well, George is her only parent. As I mentioned when I called you, he had a heart attack a few years ago. George is a workaholic—and the doctor wanted him to have some good physical therapy under his belt before he returned to work.” She stopped working for a moment to give the matter her full attention. “Well, George bent the rules. He would start therapy, but then find an excuse to part ways with his physical therapist of the moment. After going through eight therapists, Rachel told her father that he needed to stick with a program before he could come back to work. She is convinced that working so hard was what caused his heart attack in the first place." She offered Wyatt a smile. "I'm afraid that she's probably going to grill you to make sure that her father isn't going to try to get rid of you for some trumped-up excuse or other. If she likes you, you're going to be more than halfway there."

Wyatt grinned. "I'm not that easy to get rid of."

Theresa's eyes crinkled as she smiled at him. "I certainly hope you're right. Now, can I feed you before I send you off on this endeavor?"

"That's not necessary," he protested, although he was tempted.

"Maybe not for you," she allowed. "But for me, it's a different story. I'd feel better about this whole thing if I sent you off on a full stomach."

Theresa didn't have to bend his arm, he thought. "I never argue with a lovely woman."

She smiled at him. "Oh, you'll do, Wyatt Watson. You'll definitely do just fine. Come," she said, beckoning him to follow her into a small dining area. "Follow me to where the magic happens."

"Magic?" Wyatt questioned, amused.

"Magic," Theresa repeated. She prided herself on all the dishes she created. "I see that you and I need to get better acquainted, Wyatt."

"I am definitely looking forward to that happening," he said as he followed her to where "the magic" happened.

Chapter Three

Rachel sighed, looking around the restaurant one last time to make sure she hadn't forgotten anything in her haste to get back home.

It seemed to her that these days she was always trying to catch up. Ever since her father had had his heart attack, she had decided to remain home so that she could handle everything until he was back on his feet. Rachel had categorically refused to believe that her father wasn't going to recover, but she felt as if she was forever running behind by at least several hours, if not an entire day.

She had made up her mind to catch this

Wyatt person off guard and meet him while the man was working with her father. This way, he wouldn't be expecting her and she could see for herself just how good he really was.

As usual, the restaurant ended up demanding more of her time than she had anticipated. So, instead of eleven o'clock the way she had initially planned, it was almost twelve and she was still finding things that needed her last-minute attention.

Finally, she felt as if she was ready to leave. "Okay, you're in charge, Johanna," she said, addressing Johanna Donnelly.

Johanna's husband, a soldier, had been killed overseas years ago, and Rachel's father had hired the woman despite the fact that she had absolutely no experience in anything except being kindhearted. Once hired, Johanna did her best not to ever make George regret his decision. She was loyal to a fault and could be counted on to work whatever hours were needed. Eventually, she had risen in the ranks and was now the assistant manager. But she never got in Rachel's way.

Rachel thought of her more as family than as her father's employee.

Johanna smiled at Rachel. "Yes, I know. We've already covered that. Twice," the tall, thin woman added with a wink. "Go," she urged. "Go check out this therapist. Make sure that dad of yours isn't pulling your leg."

Rachel nodded her head. Johanna knew her father as well as she did, and was aware he could say and do anything just to get back to the place he loved so dearly: the restaurant that he had initially started with his wife and that he now felt gave his life meaning.

"Okay, I'm going," Rachel said. And then she thought of one more point she wanted to cover. Turning on her heel, she said, "Oh—"

"No, no 'oh,'" Johanna told the little girl whom she had watched grow up over the years. Placing her slender, capable hands against Rachel's back, she gently pushed the young woman toward the front door. "Go," she ordered sternly.

Rachel sighed, knowing that her father's assistant was right. She needed to get going. "Okay, okay, I'm going."

"You won't mind if I walk you to your car and watch you pull out of the parking lot, will you?" Johanna asked, still pushing Rachel toward the front door and matching her step for step.

Rachel attempted to turn around and look at the woman behind her. "Don't you trust me?"

"Rachel..." Johanna looked at her with unmistakable affection. "I *know* you," she said as if that answered the question and left no doubt.

"You have a way of getting caught up in things. Don't worry. Everything is under control here. You just make sure that this therapist is the real deal *and* that your father hasn't found a reason to fire him the way he has all those others."

Rachel smiled. Johanna definitely knew how her father operated. He was a very good man, but when he made up his mind about something, he was maddeningly stubborn.

"You're right," Rachel agreed. "I'm on my way." She glanced at her watch. Her eyes widened as the time registered. "Oh, Lord, how did it get to be so late?"

Johanna laughed. "In my experience, that usually happens one minute at a time, dear. One minute at a time."

True to her word, Johanna accompanied the owner's daughter not just to the parking lot, but right up to Rachel's aging secondhand sports car.

"You know you can go back in now. You don't have to watch me go," Rachel told the woman.

"Yes, I do," Johanna replied complacently. And she remained just there, her arms crossed before her chest, until Rachel drove out of the parking lot.

Rachel could still see the woman in her rearview mirror until she turned into the street. The second she was on the road, Rachel pressed down on the gas pedal.

Hard.

She would have liked to get annoyed with Johanna, but she couldn't, not with a clear conscience. The woman was right. If Johanna hadn't insisted that she be on her way, Rachel would have still been there, verbally checking things off a list she carried around perpetually in her head. She kept a list because she knew how much the restaurant meant to her father—and to her—but nothing meant as much as making sure that her father got back to being his former self.

Rachel abruptly blew out a breath, forcing herself to come to a stop at the traffic light. Preoccupied, she had almost gone right through it.

She pressed her lips together, silently upbraiding herself. She couldn't allow herself to get distracted like this. Her father had given her quite a scare, but with any luck, all that was now in the past.

Still, she wasn't about to be lax and let her father go back to working in the restaurant full-time unless he followed every single condition that the doctor had laid down for him.

There was no question that Rachel dearly loved her father and she knew how much the restaurant meant to him, but she wasn't going to give in and let him come back to work until she felt that he was 110 percent back to his old self—not even just 100 percent but a 110, she thought with a smile.

Driving quickly and barely squeaking through lights that were in the process of turning red, Rachel made the trip back to her house in eleven minutes rather than the usual eighteen.

Turning her vehicle onto her block and toward her house, she was about to pull up when she suddenly hit the brakes, just in time to stop from hitting a small, jazzy-looking electric-blue sports car that was right in her usual spot.

It took a moment for her heart to stop racing. She could feel it pounding hard in her chest. Her hands were clammy as she did her best to release her grip on the steering wheel.

Wow, that was close, she thought, utterly relieved that she had managed to avoid hitting the other car.

Idiot! She directed the comment at the owner of the vehicle rather than herself. The car had to belong to the therapist. Just how bright could this guy be, parking like that? He was taking up at least half the entrance to the house.

She parked close to the intrusive vehicle, and barely pulled up her hand brake before she threw open the driver's-side door and hurried out of her car.

Far from being in the best frame of mind, she all but marched into the house and loudly declared, "You're going to need to park your car somewhere other than right at the front door."

The words were out of her mouth before she even had the opportunity to make eye contact with the newest therapist that the agency had sent over.

"Sorry," she heard a deep male voice apologize from the next room. "I didn't want to be late. There was a three-car collision on the freeway on my way over here. I was afraid I was going to miss my appointment. It won't happen again," the man promised.

Her father's therapist paused to turn around and looked at her over his shoulder, adding sincerity to his apology.

The moment she took the full impact of the man in, Rachel's breath caught in her throat. At six-two, with sky-blue eyes, slightly shaggy dark blond hair and wide shoulders, Wyatt Watson looked more like a body builder than a physical therapist.

The word *gorgeous* flashed through her mind before she could stop it.

Rachel had to remind herself to breathe again.

It took her a moment before she could go through the motions of doing just that. Belatedly, as silence continued to hang heavily between them, she realized it was her turn to respond, or at least to say *something.*

Her mouth felt bone-dry as she tried to form words. Finally she told him, “That’s all right, just try to remember to park off to the side next time you come.”

Or at least she thought she said that.

Maybe the words were just echoing in her mind but unable to materialize. She caught her father looking at her, the corners of his mouth curving in amusement. What was that all about, she wondered.

Meanwhile, Wyatt was putting his hand out to her, a warm smile on his lips. “Maybe we should start fresh. I’m Wyatt Watson.”

“Yes, I know.” It took her a long moment to snap out of the haze that was floating around her brain. “I’m Rachel—Fenelli.”

The smile on his lips widened, making her knees feel like pudding.

“Yes, I know,” Wyatt said. “Your dad told me your name.”

At the mention of her father, Rachel managed to come alive a little more. Her father. Of course.

Her eyes darted toward George for half a second before returning to the therapist.

"My father," she echoed. "How is he doing?" She made prolonged eye contact with her father, the reason she had come racing home in the first place.

Her father seemed completely at ease, which was a pleasant change. Normally, in this kind of situation, he couldn't wait until the therapist of the moment was on their way out the door.

Maybe this would work out after all, Rachel thought. Maybe after a total of eight therapists, they finally had a winner.

A wave of relief washed over her.

Both her father and the therapist were looking at her right now, as if waiting for her to make some sort of a response.

C'*mon, Rach, this is no time to suddenly go brain-dead.*

"How is he doing?" she repeated a bit haltingly at first. "My father's been dying to get back to work, but I'm afraid that if he does and if it's too soon, he's going to wind up having another heart attack," she said to the therapist honestly, her voice lowering just a shade.

Rather than answer her, Wyatt nodded his head to the side, indicating that they should take the conversation over there.

To her surprise—and relief—her father didn't look offended or impatient. He remained where he was. This Wyatt Watson really did seem to have a good effect on him.

Eager to obtain some sort of a response—hopefully a positive answer—from Wyatt, she opened her mouth to urge him on. But before she could say anything further, Wyatt quietly told her, "While there's always a chance—a slim one—that your father might take a step backward, you must know that he appears to be a very strong man, not to mention stubborn," he added with a smile.

It pleased her that he seemed to have such a good handle on her father. *At least the stubborn part*, she thought. She began to feel hopeful. "Oh, he is that."

"Well, stubbornness can actually be a good thing," Wyatt said. "Trust me, there's nothing worse than a patient just throwing up their hands and saying that they can't do something, or they aren't up to it. Stubbornness is what gets them out of a funk, not to mention that it helps them with the exercises."

Rachel was trying to understand what Wyatt was telling her and put it in perspective. It made a lot of sense to her. Glancing back at her father's happy expression, she felt exceedingly heartened. It seemed as if the physical therapist was on the right path and her father appeared to be sold on it.

"Then you're saying you think he'll be able to go back to work?" she asked.

"Part-time," Wyatt interjected. "I'd say that he can definitely go back on a part-time basis as long as he promises not to overdo it."

Rachel laughed. She'd been down that route before, more than once. "Ah, easier said than done."

"It's all in the way you say it. And he does understand the ramifications, you know. As for now," Wyatt went on, turning his attention back to her father, "would you like to see your dad go through some of the exercises we have been working on?"

He made it sound like a joint venture, but she knew better. There was nothing she would have liked more than to see her father exercising and making progress, but there was a slight problem with that.

"I would, but Dad might feel uncomfortable having me look on," Rachel said honestly.

"I think his pride of accomplishment might just outweigh his sense of embarrassment," Wyatt said. And then he stepped back. "But it's entirely up to you."

She appeared undecided for a moment, then, making up her mind, she crossed the floor back over to her father.

Rather than any trendy workout attire—which Rachel had gotten her father in order to motivate him—George was wearing a sleeveless sweatshirt and a pair of nondescript sweatpants.

She smiled at him. "I hear you're doing well, Dad."

George looked beyond his daughter's shoulder at Wyatt. He had to admit that he was a little uneasy about this whole venture, but once he had met the young man—who hadn't a clue that this was anything more than just a professional engagement of his services—he was well pleased with the choice that his old friend had made. Nothing he had heard about Maizie and her friends' matchmaking venture was an exaggeration.

For the first time since he had found himself lying in that hospital bed, hooked up to all those wires and tubes that threatened to turn his active lifestyle into that of an inert vegetable, George Fenelli felt real hope. Hope that everything he had ever wanted for his daughter—a career in nursing and more important, a thoughtful, caring man to love her—was more than a possibility. Going back to work was just icing on the cake.

"For the first time, I think I am," George told her after a beat and it wasn't just for the sake of the part he was playing. He truly meant it. Then, taking a breath, he asked, "Do you want to stick around and see what this newest slave driver has me doing?"

For a moment, the question caught her off guard. Worded the way it was, she thought her father was being resentful again. And then she saw the sparkle in his green eyes. He actually *liked* the physical therapist who had been assigned to him this time.

Suddenly, she felt a real surge of optimism. If her father liked this man, then maybe, just maybe he would try to go through the paces that the therapist set for him and do the exercises that the man felt were called for. At any rate, that meant that her beloved father would eventually be his normal old self again.

A huge wave of cheer swelled in her heart.

It was going to be all right.

"I'd love to, Dad," she said, drawing a chair over so she could watch him and not be in either man's way. Her eyes sparkling, she urged, "Go for it."

Chapter Four

Rachel stuck around for a while, watching Wyatt interact with her father. She was impressed that even though it was his first time with her father, he patiently reviewed a series of exercises with him.

Her father did better than she had expected. The exercises were simple. None of them were really strenuous on the surface. However, Rachel had a feeling that once they were put together, they would have the desired effect. Little by little—if he kept up with them—the exercises would get her father back on the road to complete recovery—or as complete as humanly possible.

She told herself that she wasn't hoping for miracles—but the plain truth of it was that she actually was—because it meant so much to her father. And even after all this time, the restaurant still didn't seem the same without him.

In her judgment, Wyatt seemed competent enough but she had to admit that he was too damn good-looking. She couldn't shake off the notion that he had been sent from Central Casting rather than an actual physical therapy firm.

You're letting your imagination run away with you, Rachel chided herself.

All in all, given the circumstances, Rachel would have wanted to remain longer. However, as usual, there was a whole list of things she still had to see to at the restaurant if it was to retain its reputation as well as continue to bring in money. When she caught herself staring at Wyatt for the third time instead of watching her father do his exercises, she decided that it was time to get going.

As discreetly as possible, Rachel rose to her feet and picked up her shoulder purse. The second she did, both men stopped interacting and turned to look in her direction in unison.

"Sorry," she apologized, flushing slightly,

"But I'm afraid I have to be getting back to the restaurant."

Her father nodded. He was the last person she needed to explain herself to. Moreover, her dedication warmed his heart and he waved her on.

"Go, go," he urged his daughter.

For his part, Wyatt looked somewhat surprised. It was obvious that he had assumed she would stay longer, possibly throughout the rest of the session.

But then, he did understand that work could be a demanding mistress. His certainly was.

In a way, that gave them something in common.

"I'm just planning on doing more of the same," Wyatt told her, thinking that might make this easier for her. "Each session, we'll be adding a few more exercises to the workout so that it begins to feel easier and easier."

To emphasize his point, he took out a blue folder from his briefcase and held it up. He kept a collection of exercises in the folder, each providing detailed steps of the exercises so that his patients would know precisely what to do with each one as it came up.

Peeking over her shoulder, her father glanced at some of the exercises. He didn't bother stifling a groan.

The sound made Rachel laugh. "Perfect."

She was clearly delighted and handed the folder back to Wyatt. In her opinion, the collection was wonderful and it appeared that her father's physical therapist was on to something.

Maybe the man wasn't just another pretty face.

Pausing to kiss her father's cheek before she left, Rachel told him, "Follow Wyatt's instructions and maybe, just maybe I'll let you come back to the restaurant sooner than later."

And then she turned toward the physical therapist for just a second. "Thank you," she told the man, smiling at him warmly.

The next moment, Rachel turned on her heel and was out the door before Wyatt had a chance to say anything in response.

Wyatt shook his head. "Your daughter certainly moves fast."

George saw the admiring look in Wyatt's eyes. He could have sworn he was aware of sparks flying between his daughter and the handsome physical therapist.

Yes! he thought. *Bless you, Maizie.*

Out loud, George replied with a soft, pleased laugh, "You don't know the half of it." Then, just in case his comment made Wyatt wonder what was going on, George continued with his story. "Luckily, Rachel takes after her mother. That makes her very resilient. Otherwise I'm not all that sure she would have survived." He saw Wyatt looking at him curiously. "I raised her after her mother left us."

George realized that Wyatt might have gotten the wrong impression. At the very least, the therapist might have thought that there had been an acrimonious divorce involved. He wanted to set the record straight.

George told Wyatt in a very quiet voice, "My wife died."

"Yes, I know," Wyatt said quickly.

"You know?" George questioned, surprised.

Had Maizie told the young man about the family? But why? Had the woman confessed what she was actually attempting to accomplish by bringing Wyatt in to give him physical therapy exercises, George wondered.

That didn't sound right. After all, Maizie had told him that this whole thing was being conducted beneath a veil of secrecy, just like all the other "matches" that she and her two friends had managed to arrange in the past.

"Yes," Wyatt answered, "I try to find out as much as possible about my patient before I undertake his or her case. That gives me a clearer understanding of what I'm dealing with, as well as how to help my patient more efficiently. I don't believe in wasting time."

"Well, that's commendable," George said as he slowly raised and lowered first one leg, then the other, under the younger man's watchful eye. "But I would have thought that becoming familiar with the reason I needed a physical therapist would have given you enough information to set up the exercise program."

"I don't work that way," Wyatt told him with a smile. "You never know when the smallest detail might provide the key to an exercise that would wind up helping a patient."

George struggled not to grin from ear to ear. Right at that moment, he began to envision himself dancing at his daughter's wedding.

The moment Rachel walked into the restaurant, Johanna left what she was doing in the office and hurried to her side. The expression on the assistant manager's face was hopeful and eager.

"So do you think this new physical therapist is here to stay, or is your father going to exercise his power of veto on this one, too?"

Rachel left her purse in the small office and came out to join the assistant manager. "No, I really think that he's going to last, at least for a little while."

"He?" Johanna asked, obviously surprised.

Rachel nodded. "He," she told the woman she had known ever since she was a little girl.

"This time it appears that the agency sent a man and Dad really seems to like him—thank heavens."

Focused on doing her job even while she talked, Rachel began reviewing the checklist she had made for herself late last night.

Johanna seemed intrigued. Like Rachel, she wanted to see George fully recovered and back at work. "So what's this miracle worker like?"

The question caught Rachel off guard. She thought for a moment. The answer that sprang to her lips—"Cute"—had nothing to do with Wyatt's qualifications. Besides, it didn't matter if the man *was* cute, she had put her life on hold far too long. She had no time for "cute" or anything remotely like "cute." She needed to concentrate on the career she had let slide.

"What do you mean?" Rachel asked a tad too innocently to Johanna's way of thinking.

"Is he young, old, knowledgeable, confused? Is he good-looking or does he have a face that would stop a clock at twenty paces?" Johanna answered, wondering why Rachel needed to have that clarified.

Rachel deliberately avoided making eye contact with the older woman. Instead, she addressed the questions as matter-of-factly as possible. "Well, he's young and he seems to know what he's doing."

"What does he look like?" Johanna prodded, returning to the question she wanted answered. The question she felt that Rachel was doing her best to avoid. She couldn't help wondering why.

Still avoiding eye contact, Rachel shrugged. "He's okay," she answered vaguely.

"In other words," Johanna guessed, "he's gorgeous."

"I wouldn't say that," Rachel said quickly.

"You didn't have to. Your eyes said it for you."

"It doesn't matter what he looks like, Johanna," Rachel protested a little too strongly. "It matters what he does for Dad."

"Oh, I totally agree—but it doesn't hurt anything if he's easy on the eyes," the woman said with a smile.

At a loss, Rachel merely shrugged again. She was still rather uncomfortable with her reaction to the physical therapist. Admittedly, she hadn't responded that way to a man since Elliott.

"I see we're going to have to do this the hard way," Johanna concluded.

"We don't have to do this at all," Rachel said pointedly.

Johanna's eyes seemed to be laughing at her. "What fun is that?"

Rachel sighed. "This isn't supposed to be *fun*, Johanna. This is supposed to be about Dad getting better," she insisted. She didn't like the thought that she seemed to be so transparent. And she really didn't know why, but this was making her uncomfortable.

"Oh, absolutely," Johanna agreed easily. "But if the guy working with your dad is handsome, that isn't exactly what I'd call a deal breaker, either." She smiled brightly, adding, "I'd call that a real opportunity."

Rachel relented. "Maybe some other time and place, it would be. But right now, honestly, all I want to do is make some headway in my schoolwork."

Johanna nodded, indicating that she clearly understood—but she had an addendum. "But who's to say that you can't do both?"

Rachel looked at Johanna, clearly stunned. The woman had to be kidding, right? Hadn't Johanna been paying any attention the last couple of years as she ran herself ragged and practically into the ground just to keep the restaurant going and seeing to her father's care until he could get back up on his feet and run the restaurant on his own?

By her calculation, she was about two years behind in her sleep.

"For one thing, there are only twenty-four hours in a day and I'm already using up twenty-six and a half. I don't think I get to use any more," Rachel confessed. "I'm already burning the candle not just on both ends—but in the middle, too."

Johanna drew her aside and lowered her voice so that the rest of the staff couldn't hear her. "Honey, there's always time for a good-looking man. Because if you decide on plowing through your existence with blinders on, you'll always wonder what it might have been like if you'd paused long enough to admire the 'scenery' along the way."

"Sorry, Johanna," Rachel said as she made her way into the storage area, "I just don't have the time for that sort of thing."

"Make time," Johanna called out to her. "By the way, what's this physical therapist's name?"

"Wyatt," Rachel called back.

She could hear the woman sigh all the way to the storage area. "Wyatt what?"

"Are you thinking of getting some physical therapy?" she asked, concerned. Was Johanna keeping something from her? She wasn't by nature a complainer. Every since her father had had his heart attack, Rachel was exceedingly alert for any signs of unaddressed health problems amid her staff and that included Johanna.

"Wyatt what?" Johanna asked once again.

"Watson," Rachel answered. "Wyatt Watson." She glanced at Johanna over her shoulder. "Do you want to know his shoe size, too?"

Johanna's eyes met Rachel's. Even with this much distance between them, Rachel could see the devilish look in the woman's eyes.

"That's not the part I'm interested in," Johanna said matter-of-factly.

That gave Rachel some pause. Maybe she had completely misunderstood the situation. Maybe Johanna had decided that her father wasn't interested in her and she was looking for someone to fill the void in her own life. The poor woman had been alone for more years than she could count. Initially, Rachel had hoped, after her mother's passing, that her father and Johanna would get together.

For the first time she decided that maybe that didn't seem likely.

"He's too young for you, Johanna," she informed the assistant manager.

"Good to know," Johanna answered. "But I wasn't thinking about being the one to pair up with him," she said pointedly.

Okay, back to the first theory, Rachel thought. "Well, I'm certainly not pairing up with him," she said. And she had already wasted too much time discussing this.

"Well, if he's as cute as you say—" Johanna began, leaving her sentence hanging.

"I did not say that he was all that cute," Rachel protested.

Johanna smiled knowingly. "I read between the lines," she said with a broad wink. "And your father already likes him."

"I didn't say that—exactly," Rachel said. She was beginning to feel hemmed in. Johanna was the only person who could do that to her.

"I know your dad. If George didn't throw this Wyatt out on his ear within half an hour, that's a sign that he likes the guy."

"Be that as it may, I still don't have the time for this," Rachel insisted.

Johanna shook her head at the protest. "Remember that sixty years from now as you're sitting on some porch, rocking back and forth and wondering just what 'might have been.'"

Okay, enough was enough. She'd been polite long enough. "Any other cheerful words you want to share, Johanna?"

"Not at the moment, but I think I made my point." Walking up to Rachel, she patted her on the shoulder. "You think about that for now and we'll talk later after the lunch crowd goes."

Rachel said nothing, but she knew that after the lunch crowd dispersed, she would be busy getting ready for the dinner crowd, which was almost always even larger. Maybe Johanna would forget all about this conversation by the time the day was over.

At least she could hope.

Chapter Five

Rachel was sitting at what she had always regarded as her father's desk in the small cubbyhole of an office. When she had initially taken over her father's duties, she had found the office to be in complete turmoil. Everywhere she'd looked, things were in disarray.

There was no question that her father was a really great restaurateur, but as far as being able to keep track of filing, or being able to find *anything* within that small area, it was nothing if not an exercise in complete futility.

The first thing she had done on that sad, earthshaking day was to organize the chaos. It took her more than three days, but she'd managed to finally create order.

At this point, she knew where everything was and could easily lay her hands on anything she needed to keep the place running smoothly.

However, that still didn't stop her from feeling exhausted, like a marathon runner in the middle of her third race of the day.

Right now she was doing her weekly inventory. It kept her on her toes. She made a point of ensuring that everything that was being offered on the menu would continue to be in supply. She had made a vow to herself that no one who came to eat at the restaurant would *ever* hear the words "I'm sorry but we seem to be all out of that."

Engrossed in reviewing all the items she had noted when she had gone into the supply closet, Rachel didn't hear the knock on the office door. It was only when Johanna knocked a little more loudly the second time, and then cleared her throat, that Rachel finally heard her. Startled, she looked up.

"Sorry, I was just trying to decide if we needed to order more potatoes for next week, or if our usual number will see us through," she explained.

When she finally looked more intently at Johanna, she saw that the woman had a really wide smile on her face. Rachel instantly felt her stomach tightening. She immediately thought of her father. "My father's here, isn't he?"

It would be just like him to pop up again. Wyatt had been working with her father for three days now. Surprisingly, her father hadn't attempted to come in to work at the restaurant. He hadn't even hinted about coming in, or tried to convince her that he was up to it the way he had been doing ever since he was released from the hospital.

For three days he hadn't said a single word about coming back, which made her all the more suspicious. She was certain that the man was up to something. It was like waiting for a shoe to drop—loudly—but for three days, it hadn't.

"No," Johanna told her, "he's not. But someone else definitely is." The assistant manager's words were accompanied by one of the biggest smiles Rachel could ever remember seeing on the woman's face.

Warning signals went off in Rachel's head.

She could feel herself growing very edgy. "Johanna, I'm tired. It's been a very long day and I've still got studying to do when I get home. I don't have time for riddles. Now, if there's someone here to see me, tell me. Otherwise let me get back to making up the list for the coming week's orders."

Johanna drew closer to the desk, her hazel

eyes dancing merrily. “You didn’t tell me that he was *this* gorgeous,” the woman said with nothing short of an appreciative sigh.

Rachel frowned, confused. “I didn’t tell you *who* was this gorgeous?”

The words were no sooner out of her mouth than she realized who Johanna had to be talking about. The woman had the same wicked smile on her face that she’d had before when she’d grilled her about Wyatt.

Rachel was instantly on her feet. “He’s here?” she cried, stunned. The next question that occurred to her was: Why? Why was Wyatt here? Had something happened to her father?

She glanced at her watch. Wyatt should have been finished with the therapy session a long time ago. What was he doing here?

“Oh, he is *definitely* here,” Johanna said breathily. “Unless of course one of the women who have been eyeing him hungrily when he walked in decided to throw him into a sack and run off with him.” There was now a wicked glint in her eyes.

Rachel stared at the assistant manager. “I’ve never known you to exaggerate before now, Johanna,” she said, caught utterly off guard.

The naughty look in Johanna’s eyes only grew more pronounced. “Oh, but I’m not,” she replied.

Rachel didn’t bother saying anything else. It

was obvious that the woman was clearly mesmerized by her father's physical therapist. Instead, she just moved past Johanna and walked out into the restaurant proper.

Rachel saw the man almost immediately.

Johanna was right, she thought. Even from this distance, there was no denying that Wyatt Watson was immensely captivating.

He's not captivating, she chided herself. *He's your father's physical therapist and he's totally out of place here.*

Rachel strode toward him just as Wyatt turned around to look in her direction. Their eyes met and she could have sworn there were instant sparks going off.

She had to stop listening to Johanna.

Wyatt, meanwhile, lost no time in cutting short the distance between them. "I hope you don't mind my coming in this way."

Rachel hardly heard him. Her mind was filling up with all sorts of thoughts that were creating awful scenarios in her head.

"Is my father all right? Did he have another attack?" she cried breathlessly, really afraid of what she might hear in response.

Wyatt saw that she was clearly shaken. He felt an instant stab of guilt that he might have inadvertently caused that reaction in her. He hadn't meant to add to the burden Rachel was already carrying.

"No, he's fine. Really," Wyatt assured her quickly. "When I left, your father's friend Rick had come over to spend some time with him." He smiled at her reassuringly. "Your father was showing Rick some of the exercises I had him do earlier this week."

Rachel was still looking at him uneasily. "Then my father's all right?" she asked.

"Absolutely."

Convinced that the man wouldn't lie to her when it would be so easy a thing to check out, Rachel breathed out a deep sigh of relief.

There wasn't anything wrong.

And then she stared at the physical therapist. If everything was all right, then why was Wyatt here?

She couldn't find a polite way to word her question, so she just plowed right into it. "Um, if you don't mind my asking, just why are you here?"

Rather than blurt out an answer, Wyatt looked around the area. "Would you mind if I sat down at a table? I've been on my feet all day."

She hadn't even thought of that. Where were her manners? "Oh, I'm sorry. Please, follow me," she said, and turning on her heel, led Wyatt to a small, out-of-the-way booth. "Would you like something to eat? We've got the best lasagna in the state, even if I do say so myself."

"I'm sure you do," Wyatt answered. "But I would just like a cup of coffee if you don't mind."

"Are you sure?" she asked. "It really is very good. It's my dad's secret recipe. My grandmother made quite a name for herself in Palermo making that lasagna."

Wyatt flashed her an extremely tired smile. Rachel instantly found herself thinking that the man definitely looked like she felt—except that she still had several hours of schoolwork to do after her work at the restaurant. Wyatt probably had a hopeful girlfriend waiting for him once he left—or maybe there was even a wife expecting him at home.

At that moment, it occurred to Rachel that she knew next to nothing about this man who was effectively putting her father together. All she knew was that Wyatt had certainly done a really nice job with her father, as a physical therapist.

That, and the fact that her father did seem to genuinely like Wyatt. In her opinion, that said a great deal.

"Maybe some other time," Wyatt told her politely. "Right now, I just want to get to the reason I'm here and then leave you to your work. The coffee is to keep me from falling on my face," he explained in case she was wondering about that.

Seeing one of the servers go by, Rachel raised her hand and called to the petite blonde. "Virginia, please bring one espresso for the gentleman here."

"Espresso?" Wyatt questioned a little uncertainly. "I just want coffee."

She flashed a quick smile at him. "If you want to stay awake, I promise you that espresso will do the trick. You won't be falling on your face even if you wanted to."

"I suppose this way I won't have to worry about driving home," Wyatt said, turning the idea over in his head.

Rachel laughed softly. "You might have to worry about being able to fall asleep once you get home," she cautioned with a smile. "You should drink it slowly if you're not used to it. The espresso might have you feel as if you're moving several inches off the ground."

"Your father didn't mention that you had a tendency to exaggerate," Wyatt told her.

She smiled as she looked into his eyes.

Blue.

They were electric-blue, she realized. And completely hypnotic.

She made herself look away before she began to drown in them.

"That's because I don't," she told him. "My dad's the dreamer, I'm not. I have always been the practical, grounded one."

Seeing Virginia approach with a single serving of espresso in a black demitasse cup, Rachel momentarily glanced at Wyatt. "Looks like your coffee has arrived."

Wyatt caught a whiff of the brew. "Smells strong," he commented.

Rachel grinned.

"What's so funny?" he asked, confused.

"You're lucky it's not doing push-ups," she said.

He decided that he had better get the inky dark liquid into his system before he started talking and making no sense. He had been up almost around the clock and he thought that Rachel needed to hear this while he was still coherent.

Taking a sip, he felt as if every fiber in his body suddenly stood at attention. The liquid was hot and bitter as it went down.

Rachel watched him as he drank. "So? What do you think?"

"I'm surprised you don't serve this with a knife and fork," he said. He paused as the drink slowly undulated its way down through his system.

"It's not that bad," she told him.

"I didn't say it was bad, just kind of thick,"

he clarified. "Really thick, but good," he agreed after another sip. "It kind of grows on you."

She smiled, remembering that she had said the same thing the first time she sampled the dark brew. Except she had added, "Like fungus."

He laughed when she recalled her comment. Rachel found herself thinking that he had a really nice, hearty sound that enveloped her like a warm hug. Caught by surprise, she allowed herself to enjoy it—but just for a moment.

Wyatt sipped the coffee again, then placed the cup back in its saucer. At this point, the small cup was close to empty. It had only been a small amount, but he felt as if he was really wired.

"Why aren't you having any?" he asked.

Not wanting to launch into any explanations, she merely said, "I'll have mine a little later, when I go home."

Wyatt glanced at his watch. That would be pretty late, he estimated. He would have thought she'd want to experience the lift now, while she was working.

"Won't that keep you up?" he asked. He wasn't sure if the tiny cup he'd just had wouldn't wind up doing the same thing to him, since this was a totally new sensation for him.

She smiled wearily, more to herself than at Wyatt. "That's the idea," she replied.

He could only think of one reason for that. "Big date?" he asked, then immediately withdrew his question. "Sorry, none of my business."

Wyatt figured that it was the polite thing to say, although he did find himself wondering about this dynamo who had taken over her father's business at the drop of a hat. Someone else might have just opted to sell rather than change her life around to keep her father's restaurant going.

"No, it's not," Rachel agreed, although she was surprised he said it so readily. "But in the interest of being polite, I'll say my drinking espresso has nothing to do with a big date—or even a little one. Unless you think of online classes as a date."

A light went off in Wyatt's head as he remembered a pertinent detail. "Oh, that's right. Your dad mentioned something like that to me. Mainly, though, he talked about how guilty he felt that you had put your whole life on hold just for him."

Rachel closed her eyes, searching for patience. Wyatt caught himself wondering if she closed her eyes like that when she was kissed. The next second he roused himself. That wasn't the kind of thought he should be having—at least, not at this point.

"He has nothing to feel guilty about," Rachel insisted. "I wouldn't have been able to live with myself if I had gone off to college while my father was lying in a hospital bed. If he has anything to feel guilty about, it's for being such a good father that he left me no choice but to stay to make sure he was on the road to recovery."

She watched the physical therapist as she allowed herself to share something personal with the man. Who knew, maybe it would even help Wyatt understand her father more clearly.

"If I had left for school, everything would have crumbled and gone to hell in the proverbial handbasket. Besides—" she gestured about "—I love this restaurant almost as much as he does. I grew up here." A fond smile curved her lips. "My very best memories are all centered here."

Rachel suddenly realized that maybe she *was* talking too much. She pressed her lips together.

"You said you came here for a reason," she said, getting back to her initial question. "What did you want to see me about?"

Wyatt smiled, slightly embarrassed that he had gotten so off topic. "Sorry, this liquid brew just seemed to chase everything else out of my head. I wanted to talk to you about your father."

She did her best not to sigh, but she did brace herself, thinking that she probably wasn't going to like wherever this was going. She loved him dearly, but that didn't change the fact that her father had a tendency to be very trying.

"Okay, just give it to me straight. What has he done?" Then, before Wyatt could answer, she quickly launched into an apology. "If my dad insulted you in any way, he really didn't mean it."

She moved in a little closer without realizing it—although Wyatt did. He liked the closer proximity.

"To be honest, out of all the physical therapists he's had," Rachel went on, "you have turned out to be the best one by far. And that's not just me saying it. He sings your praises every night the moment I drag myself into the house."

"Well, I like him, too," Wyatt told her. "Which is why I agreed to be his go-between."

She didn't understand. "Go-between?"

Wyatt nodded. "Your father wanted me to talk to you. He didn't exactly say as much, but I did get that distinct impression."

Well, this had certainly taken an unusual turn, Rachel couldn't help thinking. "Talk to me about what?" she asked Wyatt cautiously.

"About his coming back to work almost full-time."

Chapter Six

Rachel looked at Wyatt. She was stunned and admittedly somewhat disappointed over what he had just said.

So this was why the physical therapist had come looking for her.

"I see," she murmured, nodding her head. Her eyes narrowed. "So what did he promise you?" Rachel asked.

Wyatt had no idea what she was talking about. "Excuse me?"

"What did my father promise you if you could convince me to let him come back to work at the restaurant?"

He still didn't understand why Rachel would ask something like that. He wasn't in the habit of taking bribes. "He didn't promise me anything," Wyatt informed her.

"Oh, so you expect me to believe that you came here to ask for something that my father has been trying to get me to agree to ever since he could get out of his hospital bed?"

She could feel anger rising within her chest and struggled to keep it in check. Yelling at the man wouldn't accomplish anything.

"Well," Wyatt continued in a calm voice despite the fact that he had seen her eyes flash, "I do know how important the restaurant is to your father—we did spend a lot of time talking about it during his sessions. And I really think that returning to the restaurant would be important to his mental well-being. I told him that it was a possible goal as long as he kept up with the exercise program I've put together for him."

Wyatt didn't look as if he could be so naive—but she supposed that looks had nothing to do with it. And maybe her father *had* played on the man's sympathies. But she knew her father a lot better than this handsome physical therapist did.

Rachel shook her head. "He might say that he'll keep up with the program, but I know my father. He won't keep up with it no matter how good his intentions might be. Once he's back here at the restaurant, he'll get all caught up in running it, and that will be the end of his doing any sort of exercises. All his energies will be devoted to the restaurant."

To her surprise, Wyatt nodded his agreement. "Which is why I intend to keep on working with your father every morning—if that's all right with you."

Rachel stared at Wyatt. The man was the answer to a prayer. "All right with me?" she echoed. "Wyatt, it's *perfect* with me." This new twist was a lot to ask not just Wyatt, but the person who employed him and ran the company, as well. "Are you sure this program will be all right with your boss, because if there's a problem, I could talk to him or her and—" She watched as the smile blossomed on his face. She caught her breath, then pressed on. "What?"

"I *am* the boss," he told her.

"You?" she questioned. "You don't work for a physical therapy company?"

"No, there's just me." There was no conceit in his voice. It was just a simple fact. "I decided to go into business for myself a little less than six months ago. I found that I worked best without having someone breathing down my neck, making me account for my every move. I get a better feel for the patient that way."

That gave him a lot in common with her father, she thought. He had bought the restaurant because he liked running things on his own rather than taking orders from someone. But there was still something that was bothering her.

"All the other physical therapists who came to try to work with my father were sent over by the Albright Agency." She looked at his face. He really did look trustworthy, she decided, but looks weren't everything. "I don't remember switching."

Although she had to admit that this man had turned out to be far better suited to her father's needs and mindset than all the other physical therapists she had seen put together.

"Technically, you didn't," Wyatt said. "Your father is the one who made the change. From what I gather, he talked to Maizie Sommers about getting a new physical therapist. Maizie got in contact with my aunt Theresa. I was in between patients, so—"

That stopped her in her tracks. "Maizie Sommers," she repeated. "She's the one who got the wheels moving on this transfer?"

Rachel had known the real estate agent for a long time since before her mother had died. Maizie was the one who had, along with Johanna, helped her father weather those very difficult, very sad times. In all that time, Rachel had never thought about asking Maizie if she knew any good physical therapists.

"Well, in a roundabout way, yes," Wyatt admitted, further confusing her. "I don't know Maizie, but she knows my aunt Theresa—who's not really my aunt, but my cousin." He could see the confusion in Rachel's eyes growing. "It's just more respectful referring to her as my aunt because of the age difference—but the bottom line is I am a physical therapist and I did start up my own company," he told Rachel. "Eventually I want to have a few other therapists become part of the company, but right now, it's just me."

He could see that he hadn't totally convinced her. There was only one thing for him to say. "Look, if you feel that you'd rather go back to the Albright Agency because you know them, I'll totally understand."

She hadn't meant to convey that to him. And she definitely didn't want him to abandon her father. "Go back to the Albright? Oh no, no. You're the first one my father stuck it out with, the first therapist he didn't fire within twenty-four hours—or sooner," she added, remembering one incident where her father had sent the woman out the door in less than an hour. "Why would I want to go back to something that didn't work?" she asked Wyatt. "I was just afraid that my father was attempting to manipulate you.

"But apparently, that's not the case." She smiled at him. "You're very good for my father and I'd seriously consider bringing you into the family if it got you to stay on."

Wyatt laughed at the glib suggestion. "As intriguing as that sounds, that won't be necessary. A paycheck will do just fine—and perhaps a recommendation after your dad's fully recovered and I sign off on him."

The thought of Wyatt leaving made her feel unaccountably sad. She had no idea why. It didn't make any sense to her. The feeling had caught her by surprise.

"But that won't be for a while, right?" Rachel asked him.

He considered her question before he answered. "Well, I really can't be specific, but from what I can see, it's going to take a little while before I feel I can discharge your dad. I know it won't be until I am satisfied that he's fully able to carry out his duties."

They had managed to come full circle, Wyatt realized. They were now back to the question he had come to ask her in the first place. He searched her face and felt as if he had won her over. But he wasn't about to assume anything.

"So, can I tell your father that you have no objections to his coming in to the restaurant to work after we have completed his morning physical therapy session?" he asked.

She nodded. "As long as you feel that he can handle it. You know, it'll feel good not to be the 'bad guy' for a change,'" she confessed with a smile. "And it's not that I didn't want him here. It's just that I didn't want to find him crumpled on the kitchen floor again the way that I did that first time when he had that terrible heart attack and I was sure I had lost him."

Wyatt did his best to paint an encouraging scenario for her. Both she and her father needed it. "Don't worry about it. As long as he continues seeing his doctor regularly, taking his medications and doing his physical therapy sessions—also on a regular basis—your father should fare better than a lot of other men his age—or younger. I also feel that he would benefit from feeling that his life has some real meaning to it," he added. "I get the impression from him that he feels that way about running his restaurant."

Wyatt wasn't mistaken, she thought. It amazed her that he had gotten such a good handle on her father in such a short amount of time. The man was really good at his job.

"Point taken," Rachel agreed. "Listen, I have to be getting back to my duties," she told him, nodding toward the main restaurant area, "but you should feel free to stay here as long as you like. Order whatever you like for dinner."

It occurred to him that what he would like wasn't on the menu. The next moment he cautioned himself that thinking like that could easily make him lose the ground he had just managed to gain. Mixing work with pleasure was never a good idea.

So he smiled at her, reminding Rachel, "I've already turned that kind offer of yours down."

"Yes," she agreed, remembering. "But that offer was tendered more than fifteen minutes ago, before we had our nice chat. I thought that all this talking might have made you hungry."

Actually, he was hungry. But he didn't want to eat alone and she had made it obvious that she had things to do.

Wyatt rose to his feet. "Maybe some other time," he told her. "I'll take a rain check."

There was no question about it, Rachel thought. Wyatt Watson had a thousand-watt smile. And dimples, heart-melting dimples. The man got better-looking every time she saw him.

Mind back on your work, Rach. You've got a restaurant to run and a class to go to after that. You don't have time to moon over a Greek god with sky-blue eyes and knee-weakening dimples. Get your degree first. Enough time has gone by.

"Deal," she agreed. "Feel free to stop by for some bracing espresso whenever the need hits you."

His eyes met hers just before he took his leave. "It's a deal," he promised as he walked away.

"You chased him away?" Johanna asked.

Rachel jumped, then swung around, her hand over her pounding heart. "Were you hiding behind a column, eavesdropping all this time?" she cried.

"I just happened to be in the area," Johanna said innocently.

"Right," Rachel scoffed.

"So is it true?" Johanna asked, unable to contain her curiosity.

"Is what true?"

There was no mistaking the delighted look on the assistant manager's face. "That your dad's coming back to Vesuvius?"

Rachel gazed off in the general direction that Wyatt had taken when he left the restaurant. "Well, it looks that way," she answered. She certainly hoped that the physical therapist hadn't been too optimistic when he tried to convince her that her father could come back to work.

Johanna's face lit up even more than it usually did. "I *knew* I liked that young man the first time I saw him," she exulted.

Johanna had a big heart and always found something to like about everyone. It was in her general nature.

"You liked Elliott the first time you saw him, too," Rachel reminded the woman.

Unfazed, Johanna shrugged. "A person is entitled to one mistake in their lives. The important thing is to learn from it, not dwell on it."

Rachel laughed shortly, shaking her head. There was no way that Johanna ever saw anything in a really bad light. Everything always turned into something that came with a positive promise. That was one of the woman's best qualities.

"I've got to get back to making the list of supplies to order before I leave." Rachel hesitated, looking at the assistant manager. She had already asked once, but it didn't hurt to ask a second time. "Do you think you can close up tonight?"

"I don't *think*," Johanna replied, observing how much the girl was like her father. "I *know.* I can also finish up that inventory list for you."

Rachel didn't like putting too much responsibility on someone else's shoulders. It made her feel as if she was dropping the ball.

"That's okay, Johanna, I've got this," she assured her.

Johanna gave her a penetrating look. "Just remember, that was what your father kept saying. But sometimes, it's a good thing to take it easy—" her smile turned wicked "—unless, of course it involves Mr. Easy-on-the-Eyes."

Rachel shook her head. The woman never gave up. "Down, Johanna. Yes, the man is good-looking, but I am not in the market for a man—*any* man."

Johanna's expression turned serious. The woman had felt really bad for her when Elliott ended up marrying someone he had met in college. She would have scratched his eyes out if she could. "Rachel, don't let one really bad experience sour you on the idea of all men. To be very honest, your father never cared for Elliott to begin with—and neither did I," she said, surprising Rachel. "The man's world centered only around himself. You came in a distant second. Would you really have wanted to spend the next ten to twenty years with someone like that?"

Rachel sighed as the whole experience came vividly back to her, both the tears as well as the anger.

"No, of course not." She knew that now, but at the time she'd felt as if she had been sucker punched right in the stomach.

"That's my girl," Johanna said, giving her a quick hug. "If you ask me, he did you a favor. Now you're free to focus your attention on a *real* man."

"You have people lining up at the hostess table," Rachel pointed out, wanting to change the subject. "I'll call this in—" she indicated the inventory list she had compiled of the supplies the restaurant needed for the following week "—and then go. I'll see you in the morning."

Johanna nodded. "Don't worry about a thing," she told Rachel. "And see about getting to sleep earlier than five in the morning."

"I'll do my best." Rachel knew she sounded as if she was just paying lip service, but the truth of it was that she wound up staying up later far more often than she was happy about.

It wasn't that the online classes were difficult; it was just that she was really trying to absorb every nuance of every class. To her, her mother had been the ultimate nurse and she was determined to be every bit as good as she could be. She honestly didn't believe that she could be better than her mother had been. But she didn't want to bring any shame to her mother's memory.

That required a great deal of work. Hard work had never frightened her. However, she would have loved to get more than a few minutes' sleep at night.

Well, as long as she didn't fall asleep driving home, she'd be all right. It was one thing to lay her head down on her arms at the computer; it was quite another to suddenly realize that her eyes were closed as she was driving.

Feeling the haze of sleep coming over her, she debated pulling over to the side of the road for a quick nap. But if she did that, who knew how long she'd wind up sleeping? And she knew her father would be waiting for her to get in from the restaurant. If she took a nap on the side of the road, even a short one, he'd really be worried that she was late.

Even if she called to tell him what she was doing, she knew that he would be worried. More than that, he'd tell her that he was coming to get her. It wouldn't matter if she told him not to; she knew he'd come anyway.

Though his doctor had given him a clean bill of health, he was her dad and she intended to protect him at all costs. They were alike like that, she and her father, Rachel thought—except she was healthy and it wasn't all that long ago that he hadn't been.

She searched for a way to keep awake.

Unaccountably, Wyatt's image flashed through her mind. And then it came to her. She'd just think about the physical therapist until she could get home. She could focus on how much good he was already doing to her father's well-being.

It was really fortunate, she thought, that her father had stumbled across the real estate agent, telling her his problem. He probably complained about how she was being so stubborn, refusing to let him go back to his beloved restaurant until he fulfilled the physical therapy sessions his cardiologist felt he needed to do in order to get back to his old self.

Heaven bless Maizie, she thought.

Before she knew it, Rachel was home.

Chapter Seven

Her father was waiting up for her, or at least that appeared to have been his initial intention. George Fenelli was sitting, slightly slumped, in his favorite recliner.

She could remember sitting in his lap as a little girl as he sat in that chair. Remembered having her father read stories to her until she would finally fall asleep, at which point he would carry her upstairs and put her in her bed.

Now it seemed to be his turn to fall asleep in that chair. The TV was on, obviously in an effort to keep him awake. A rerun of an episode from an old comedy series called *Hunting With*

Harry, which he used to enjoy watching with her mother, was playing in the background. But the show had apparently lost its audience. Her father was sound asleep.

Rachel was tempted to just let him go on sleeping, but she knew that if he continued to doze sitting up in that position, every bone in his body would be really aching by morning—or whenever he did finally wake up.

Although she dreaded waking him up, she knew it would be kinder to do that and send him off to his bed where he could get a decent night's sleep than just to leave him here, slumped over like this.

She stood over him for a moment, smiling to herself. This had to be what it was like to have kids. Waking them up to go upstairs to their rooms after they had fallen asleep in front of the television set.

Very gently, she placed her hand on his shoulder and shook him just a little. When he didn't open his eyes, she shook a little harder.

She did it two more times until her father finally opened his eyes.

"Hi, sleepyhead," Rachel said fondly.

Her father roused himself, blinking. "Rachel," he murmured, pulling himself up in the recliner. "I've been waiting for you."

"Well, it looks like the excitement of anticipating my arrival was too much for you and you fell asleep," she said with a laugh.

"I didn't fall asleep," her father protested with feeling. "I was just resting my eyes."

Her grin grew. "Seems like you rested your eyes very well. It took me three tries to get you to open them," she said. "Now let's see about getting you upstairs so you can put that bed of yours to good use."

She had put in a great deal of research, looking for the best bed to get for her father after his surgery. He had even commented that when he was on it, it was like sleeping on a cloud.

"Says the girl who sleeps on her keyboard," her father scoffed.

"*Woman*, Dad," she corrected her father patiently, not for the first time. "I'm a woman."

"Maybe to other people, but to me, you'll always be my little girl," George said. "So you just might as well stop fighting it. I'm an old dog. I've learned all the new tricks I'm going to learn."

She knew better, but she was way too worn out to argue. "Yes, Dad."

George nodded. "That's better. And for the record, I didn't fall asleep. Only old men fall asleep in front of the TV. I'm not an old man."

She refrained from pointing out that he had just referred to himself as an old dog. If she were being honest, she really didn't like thinking of her father in that light. Part of her wanted to believe that he would go on forever. But that heart attack had really scared her right down to her toes.

Rachel didn't even want to begin to imagine what life would have been without him had he not recovered.

"No, you're not an old man," she agreed. "Which is why I've been after you to listen to the doctor and do your physical therapy sessions faithfully. They can only help you be young."

Without realizing it, Rachel had given him an opening and he definitely intended to use it to his advantage. "Speaking of physical therapy," he began as he slowly made his way to the staircase.

Rachel braced herself, knowing what was coming. "Yes?"

Her father stopped moving toward the stairs and looked at her. "Is that a 'Yes, go on talking'? Or the yes I've been trying to get you to say ever since I came home from the hospital?"

Rachel debated drawing this dialogue out and making her father wait for an answer. It would have served him right for what he had put her through. But, by the same token, she liked seeing her father happy, and there was no question that he did look happy as he stood there, waiting for a positive answer.

"Let's just say that Wyatt Watson is a very persuasive man who knows how to present facts in just the right light," Rachel told him.

George's green eyes sparkled, and for one precious moment, he looked exactly like the man in the wedding photo, standing next to the laughing, happy bride who had been her mother.

"Then it's yes?" he asked eagerly.

"It's yes—but with a condition," she quickly injected, wanting him to be aware that there were two sides to this bargain. "The second you stop keeping up your end of this and let your physical therapy sessions start to slide, the deal is off. Do you understand?"

Her father sighed. "Yes, I understand. You know, you're every bit as hard a taskmaster as your mother was."

The observation just made Rachel smile. "I take that as a compliment."

"You would," her father chuckled. His smile just widened. "Well, I guess I'll go off to bed as my taskmaster demands." And then he paused, looking at his daughter. "What about you?" he asked. "Are you going to go to bed, too?"

She only wished. "Dad, you know I have online classes to catch up on."

He frowned. "Being a nurse isn't going to do you any good if you run yourself into the ground putting in all these hours studying for it."

She knew he meant well and that he cared, but this was something she had already lost too much time trying to achieve. "I'll be fine, Dad."

George eyed her skeptically. "You'll be the girl with a permanent keyboard imprint on her face if you're not careful," he warned.

"You do have a vivid imagination, Dad," Rachel told him.

He stopped just at the base of the stairs. "Promise me that you'll get some sleep before midnight," he requested seriously.

Despite the fact that she felt really drained right now and would have loved to crawl into bed, she didn't want her father overthinking this, or worrying about her. She could take care of herself.

"Hey, if Cinderella could stay up until after midnight," she laughed, "so can I."

"Cinderella had a fairy godmother," her father pointed out.

"And I have you," she countered cheerfully, patting his cheek affectionately as she drew closer. "If you ask me, I was the one who got the better end of the deal. Now go to bed, Dad, and let me get to my classes. I've got a lot to catch up on and a lot of classes to make up."

"I'm sorry about that," he apologized with sincerity.

The expression on her father's face made her feel guilty. She hadn't meant it that way. She was just thinking of the actual online classes that she hadn't managed to absorb yesterday.

"That wasn't meant as a dig, Dad. That was just a simple fact," she told him. She appealed to his sense of logic. "Now, the more time I spend talking to you—much as I love it—the more time I'm going to have to make up for in 'class.'"

"Message received." George bent over from where he was standing and kissed her temple. "Good night, light of my life."

"Good night, Difficult Dad," she teased with a straight face.

George pretended to shake his head and lamented, "No respect," as he went up the rest of the way to his room.

Rachel waited until she heard her father's bedroom door close, then hurried up the stairs to her own room. Flipping on the light switch, she walked inside and then settled in at her desk in front of her computer.

She had every intention of putting in at least a

couple of hours of studying, if not more. But try as she might, she found that she really couldn't concentrate. Even though she was reviewing facts she already knew, they just seemed to drift through her brain without sticking.

Between feeling really exhausted and having images of Wyatt unaccountably pop up in her head when she least expected it, Rachel found herself reading the same words over and over again without having them make any sense at all—or even penetrating her brain.

Not only that, but it felt as if every bone in her body ached from all the work she had put in today at the restaurant.

There was no doubt about it, even though she would never admit it out loud to anyone—she was pushing herself too hard.

This was an exercise in futility. In addition, it had never happened to her before. She was usually able to absorb at least a little bit of information before her brain surrendered and called it quits.

However, tonight the battle seemed lost before it was even undertaken. If she was being honest with herself, her eyes had started to close the moment she sat down in front of the computer.

There was no point in beating her head against the wall, Rachel told herself.

Maybe tomorrow would be better, she hoped.

With that thought uppermost in her mind, she lay down and curled up on her bed. She was sound asleep less than five minutes after her head hit the pillow.

Rachel's inner alarm clock woke her up at the usual time, not any later, not any earlier. She had been that way ever since she had gone to first grade. All she had to tell herself was what time she wanted to wake up and she just did. There had never been a need to set an actual alarm clock. The power of suggestion took care of all that.

As soon as she was up, guilt over last night's missed lesson set in. She couldn't allow that to become a habit. She would have to find some way to make up for that after work, Rachel promised herself as she quickly hurried into her shower stall.

Maybe if she went in earlier to work and everything went smoothly for a change, she could do some studying at lunch and catch up with the rest of the missed lesson when she got home tonight.

At least that sounded like a plan. Moving at her usual fast pace, Rachel was dressed and ready to go in ten minutes. Preoccupied, she didn't hear the voices in conversation until she was almost at the bottom of the stairs.

At first she thought her father had the radio on, or maybe even the small television set he kept in the kitchen and turned on for occasional company.

But then she listened and heard a deep, baritone voice. A voice she could have sworn belonged to Wyatt.

No, it couldn't be, Rachel insisted to herself. She just had Wyatt on the brain, that was all.

In a state of denial, she walked into the kitchen. And stopped dead.

Wyatt was standing there, his back to the doorway, and from what she gathered, he was in the middle of fending off her father's invitation to eat breakfast.

"Wyatt?" she asked uncertainly, wondering why the man was here so early. From what she had picked up, the physical therapist didn't usually get here until ten o'clock in the morning.

At the sound of her voice, both Wyatt and her father looked in her direction.

Her father was the one who spoke first. "Maybe you can talk Wyatt into having breakfast," he said, appealing to his daughter. "After all, he got here incredibly early and this way he won't have to wait while I make breakfast for you and me."

She was still trying to sort things out. "What are you doing here so early?" she asked. That hadn't been their arrangement. Had things changed around for some reason?

"I thought your father and I could start our routine early," Wyatt explained easily, not missing a beat. "This way, he can arrive at the restaurant closer to the time he used to get in."

Obviously her father hadn't told Wyatt everything. In his mind, to do so would have been bragging. "Then you would have had to have been here at least a couple of hours ago," she told Wyatt. "Dad believes in getting an early start—just slightly before the rooster got up."

"I'm beginning to understand why your father had that heart attack," Wyatt said, looking pointedly at his patient.

"She's exaggerating," George protested, looking far from pleased about the nature of his daughter's narrative.

"No, I'm not," Rachel insisted, "and you know it." Rachel smiled at her father fondly. She was only keeping after him for his own good.

George made a dismissive noise and turned toward Wyatt.

"About that breakfast," he prodded, thinking

he stood a much better chance of getting the man to eat than he had of winning an argument with his daughter.

To George's delight, Rachel was apparently backing him up.

"You might as well say yes, Wyatt. My father's not going to give up until you do. Unlike me," she added with a wide smile, "the man doesn't retreat."

"What's this about you *ever* retreating?" George asked his daughter incredulously. Then, as an amused sidebar, he told Wyatt, "But she's right. I don't give up. Ever." And then he focused on Rachel. "Now what's all this about you retreating?"

"When he stopped by at the restaurant last night to make the case for you going back to work if you played by the rules, I tried to convince him to stay for dinner. But I didn't have any luck. Your physical therapist just left the restaurant without taking a single bite."

"Oh, you should have stayed," George told him in all sincerity. "Rachel here is almost as good a cook as I am. I taught her everything she knows—well, almost," her father amended with a wink in Wyatt's direction. "After all, a man's got to have some secrets."

"As you can see, false modesty is obviously

not one of my father's qualities," Rachel quipped. "But Dad is the main reason that people keep coming back to Vesuvius in spades. You might as well find out what the fuss is all about sooner than later. You'll be glad that you did."

Wyatt didn't immediately agree. "And you're staying for breakfast?" he asked.

He watched her mouth curve in amusement and found himself captivated again. "Well, I guess I'll have to now," Rachel answered, "since I played it up the way I did."

"Less talking, more eating," George dictated, using the spatula in his hand like a pointer. Turning all the way around, he distributed what he'd prepared onto three plates. "It's ready."

She looked at her father, stunned. He had made three equal, tempting portions. The aroma was wonderful, but that didn't divert her from the question that sprang up in her head.

"Then you knew he was coming?" she questioned. He didn't make this much normally.

Her father flashed his lopsided smile at her. "I'm your father. I know everything," he told her matter-of-factly.

She would have appreciated a heads-up about Wyatt being there. In all likelihood, she would have left earlier to avoid running into him. Her brain still felt hazy.

Too late now, she thought philosophically. "You keep telling yourself that, Dad."

"Does it matter where I sit?" Wyatt asked, assuming that both father and daughter had seats that they tended to favor.

"Just as long as it's at the table, it doesn't really matter where. Nothing's written in stone. Rachel and I are both flexible people," George cheerfully told the physical therapist.

Wyatt could have sworn that there was a twinkle in George's eye as he placed his plate next to Rachel's. He might have had a choice when it came to having breakfast, but it was plain that his patient had made that choice for him.

With a smile, Wyatt sat down.

Chapter Eight

Wyatt wasn't really thinking about the food that his patient had made and placed before him when he started eating. Breakfast was just something to keep his stomach from rumbling. So when the taste suddenly snuck up on him, exploding on his tongue and catching him totally off guard, he was more than a little surprised.

Wyatt heard himself blurting out the first words that came to his mind.

"Hey," he cried, "this is really good." There was no missing the enthusiasm in his voice.

Rachel's father had taken his seat directly opposite Wyatt. The note of surprise in Wyatt's voice obviously amused him. He smiled at the young man, clearly pleased. He never took a compliment for granted. No matter how many times he had heard it voiced before.

"Did you expect me to poison you?" George asked, smiling at him.

"No, of course not," Wyatt replied. "But I just expected this to taste like, well, breakfast," he said with a shrug. "Nothing out of the ordinary. And certainly nothing to make my taste buds stand up and cheer." He grinned. "Bar none, this is probably the best breakfast I have ever eaten—no offense to my mother."

"Well, I won't tell her if you won't," George promised with an unexpected twinkle in his eye. And then he looked at his daughter. "I'm sure that Rachel can be trusted to keep a secret. You won't say anything, will you, honey?"

"About what?" she deadpanned, wide-eyed.

"See?" George said, looking at his therapist. "Nothing to worry about." He noted with pleasure how quickly Wyatt's breakfast was disappearing. "Do you want seconds?"

"No, this is more than enough," Wyatt assured his patient. He knew that this was far more than he usually consumed. Usually, a piece of toast would see him through to lunch. "If I have any more I won't be able to go through the paces and show you how to do those new exercises."

George looked at the French fries he'd made for Rachel that still remained in the bowl. There had to be a little less than half a bowl left. He didn't believe in pushing the food he made, but neither did he believe in just tossing food away, either.

"Well, the fries are here if you find that you've changed your mind and want them."

"I'll keep that in mind, sir," Wyatt replied good-naturedly.

Her father rose to get more coffee for himself. Rachel took the opportunity to lean in closer to Wyatt and tell him in a low, conspiratorial voice, "You realize that you've just made my father very happy." And because he did, she was very grateful to the physical therapist, and saw him in an entirely new light. "After all these years, my father still never gets tired of hearing favorable comments about his cooking. Keep that up," she said with a grin, "and he may be tempted to adopt you."

Wyatt's eyes swept over her face before he looked directly into her eyes. "I don't think that would be a very good idea," he confided in a similar whispering tone.

Rachel was caught off guard, not knowing

what to answer as she sensed what he meant by that.

Just then, her father returned with his oversize mug filled to the brim.

"You two whispering about anything I should know about?" George asked, looking at the pair as he took his seat again.

"We're just discussing how his compliment about your food made you exceptionally happy," Rachel said. Leaning over, she snagged a couple of French fries, making short work of both of them.

"Only if he meant it," George qualified, looking at the man who was putting him through his physical therapy paces.

Wyatt's expression remained serious. "I never lie."

He had already eaten too much. But considering how tasty the fries were, Wyatt could easily see himself quickly disposing of the entire portion of the remaining fries.

George nodded. "Now, there's a rarity these days. An honest man." His voice sobered. "Say, now that we've broken the ice, why don't you come by Vesuvius at the end of the week and I'll whip up one of my specialties for you. I should be in full swing by then, able to prepare my specials." And then he slanted a glance in his daughter's direction. "That is, if my warden decides to take my shackles off." He turned his attention toward Wyatt. "So what do you say?"

"Offhand, I'd say that sounds like an offer that I can't refuse," Wyatt answered with a straight face. "Provided you don't push yourself too hard and overdo it."

"Don't worry," Rachel told Wyatt. "I intend to watch my father like a hawk. He's not going to get a chance to overdo anything."

George sighed dramatically. It was only half in jest.

"You heard the warden," he lamented. "But I have to warn you that I won't be at the top of my game, making that dinner for you," he told Wyatt as if he was a fellow conspirator. And then he brightened. "Maybe when you come, you can distract her for me. Because I don't do very well when I have someone breathing down my neck—even if it is my own daughter."

Wyatt didn't bother hiding his amusement. His patient had just used the same wording that he had when he'd tried to explain to his family and friends why he decided to leave the company he'd been working for and go off to start his own. Because, just like George, he found he fared a lot better without having someone breathing down his neck.

George saw the grin on Wyatt's face and felt he interpreted it correctly. He was really growing to like this young man. A lot.

Wyatt had promised to stop by and see his mother, so he took a detour on his way home. Ariel Watson had called earlier to say that she had wrenched her back. Short on details when he asked for them, all she had said was that she wanted him to suggest a few physical therapy exercises she could try.

He had to admit that he was somewhat suspicious about the whole thing. He had never known his mother to say anything positive about his chosen vocation. But despite his doubts, he felt he couldn't very well turn his back on his mother's request.

Pulling up before the old 1963 building where he and his siblings had grown up, he saw that another vehicle was parked in front of the house. He recognized it immediately. The car belonged to his sister.

Wyatt sighed. Whatever was going on, he had an uneasy feeling that he would get hit with both barrels. Part of him was sorely tempted just to turn around and drive away.

But he told himself that would just be an out-

and-out act of cowardice. Bracing himself, he parked his vehicle and forced himself to get out.

He opened the door with his spare key and walked in, calling out, "It's me, Mom. I'm here about your back. Is it still giving you trouble?"

"No, but my son is," Ariel replied, raising her voice.

And there it is, Wyatt thought, resigning himself.

His sister, Myra, joined in, calling out, "We're in the living room, Wyatt."

He should have left when he had the chance, Wyatt thought. But he kept a smile on his face as he followed the sound of his sister's voice and walked into the living room.

He nodded at Myra. Although years separated them, they looked like twins, despite Myra's decidedly blonder hair.

He saw that his mother appeared far from pleased. *Now what?* he wondered. He proceeded on as if he hadn't noticed anything. It was easier that way.

"I take it your back is feeling better," Wyatt said to her.

"Yes, but my heart isn't," his mother informed him complainingly.

"Sorry, Mom. You're going to have to see a cardiologist about that and, as you never cease to remind me, I'm not that, or any other kind of a doctor, either."

"Mom," his sister said, a warning note in her voice, "please don't get on Wyatt's case."

However, as usual, Ariel Watson didn't give the impression that she was about to back down. She never failed to speak her mind and this was no exception.

She fixed her youngest-born with a glare. "Your boss called today, asking for you."

That caught him off guard. He looked at his mother, trying to ascertain just what she was up to. She knew perfectly well that his situation had changed in the last six months.

"I don't have a boss, Mom," Wyatt patiently reminded her.

"Your *old* boss," his mother underscored, obviously irritated and far from happy about the situation. She sighed, shaking her head, the picture of the long-suffering mother.

"It was hard enough for me to accept you refusing to go to medical school, but for you to walk out on an established firm with excellent benefits the way you did—" Her voice trailed off for a moment as she dramatically shook her head. "What on *earth* were you thinking?"

"I was thinking," he said not for the first time, "that I wanted to start my own business because that is the only way for me to grow." He was doing his best to remain respectful and not raise his voice. "No offense, Mom, but we've already been through this not once but a number of times."

"But we haven't resolved it to my satisfaction," Ariel reminded her son.

And we never will, Wyatt thought. *Not until I see things her way.*

"Mom," Myra said, coming to her brother's rescue. "You're not the one who counts here. The more you push, the more Wyatt is going to ignore you and just go his own route."

"Not the way I'd put it, but that's the general gist of it," he agreed, nodding at his sister. "Now, if your back has gotten better—" He refrained from stating he figured that his mother had gotten him to come over under false pretenses, because he really didn't want to get embroiled in a more heated argument than this was already shaping up to be. "It's been a long day and I'd like to go home and get some well-deserved rest."

His sister spoke up, obviously hoping to prevent any sort of confrontation. "Since you're already here, I wanted to talk to you about something."

Wyatt usually got along well with everyone

in his family, especially his sister, but lately, she had begun pushing a particular agenda. She was focused on fixing him up with Gloria Chase, a friend of hers who had a crush on him.

He had met her once and she seemed perfectly nice, except for her habit of talking nonstop. The one time they had been thrown together at one of Myra's gatherings, Gloria didn't seem to come up for air the entire time. He really had no desire to endure that again.

If he was looking to be paired up with anyone in the immediate future, he would have far preferred it to be with Rachel.

The idea flashed through his mind and took root. Wyatt could feel his mouth curving as he thought about the idea.

Suddenly realizing that Myra might just take his smile to be encouragement, Wyatt felt it best to beg off for now.

"Could we talk about this some other time, Myra? I'm really wiped out."

Myra interpreted his words her own way. "Does that mean your client list is growing?"

Wyatt grabbed at the excuse and nodded. "It is getting bigger. And I've been working since early this morning, so—"

Although for the most part he got along well

with Myra, he began to make his way toward the door so he could make a quick getaway.

"This will be quick," Myra promised, grabbing his wrist. "As you might remember, Matthew and I are celebrating our tenth wedding anniversary next Saturday," she announced, clearly thrilled about the event, "and I just wanted to make sure that you'll be there."

"I wouldn't miss it for the world. Just text me where you're having the celebration and what time you want me to be there," he said, turning back toward the door.

"I will, and you don't have to find a date. Gloria Chase would be more than thrilled to have you bring her."

He felt his stomach tightening. Just what he didn't want to happen. His brain immediately searched for a way out.

"As a matter of fact," he said before he could think better of it, "I am seeing someone. If she's free, I'll be bringing her."

Both his mother and his sister cried, "Oh?" almost in unison as they exchanged looks.

Ariel recovered first. She shot her son a skeptical look. "You never said anything about a girlfriend," his mother accused.

"You never asked," Wyatt told her with a

smile. "Besides, you know I don't really believe in labels, Mom."

"But you could have told me," Myra lamented. Then, brightening, because she did want the best for her brother, she rallied. "What's her name? Who is she? Where did you meet?" The questions were fired at him quickly like bullets.

Wyatt shook his head. "That's why I didn't tell you. I wanted to be sure that this relationship—if that's what it turns out to be—had a chance of getting off the ground before I was subjected to a recreation of a poor man's Spanish Inquisition."

Ariel disregarded her son's quip. "So do we get to meet this woman you're in a non-relationship in?"

Wyatt couldn't tell if his mother was genuinely asking the question, or if she had decided that this was all just a big smoke screen and there really wasn't anyone to meet.

He decided to toss her a crumb, betting on the fact that Rachel had a kind heart and would bail him out when he told her what was going on.

"I said that if she's not busy, I'll be bringing her to the anniversary celebration, so yes, with any luck, you will get to meet her," Wyatt told his mother, hoping that put an end to this interrogation—at least temporarily.

For her part, Myra appeared disappointed that

she wouldn't be able to pair her brother up with her friend, but the bottom line was that she was happy her brother had finally found someone. He had been so focused on work all this time, and as far as she could tell, there hadn't been anyone in his life, at least no one serious, for a very long time.

Too long, in her opinion.

"I can't wait to meet her," Myra told her brother enthusiastically.

"Don't start celebrating just yet," Ariel warned her daughter. "Wyatt may decide to call the whole thing off and come solo." She fixed her son with a penetrating, knowing look.

"Well, if he does, Gloria will probably come alone, so the two of them would be free to join forces," Myra said with a smile. "Either way, my little brother isn't going to be alone on my anniversary." She patted his cheek. "I'll forward you all the details. And I'll see you next Saturday."

Smiling happily, Myra paused to brush her lips against his cheek.

Wyatt nodded. "I'll keep an eye out for your text," he told his sister, keeping a smile on his lips even though part of him felt as if he had just stepped in quicksand and was swiftly going under.

Feeling drained, he told himself that he

needed to get out of there. Saying his goodbyes, Wyatt added, "Glad your back's not bothering you, Mom," and quickly went out to his car before either woman could stop him.

As he got in behind the steering wheel, Wyatt felt somewhat stunned. How could he have let that lie escalate the way it had? He hadn't wanted to get fixed up with Myra's friend. He was certain that path only led to complications and hurt feelings, not to mention undoubtedly having his mother and his sister on his back.

He had only one recourse open to him. He would have to throw himself on Rachel's good graces.

Either that, or come up with one hell of a plausible excuse.

He doubted if he could come up with something that both women would buy. That meant that appealing to Rachel was his only chance.

Chapter Nine

Wyatt did his best not to think about it.

After all, Myra's anniversary was almost a full week away. A lot of things could happen within a week.

Besides, it wasn't as if he was afraid of asking Rachel to come with him to the celebration, but the fact remained that he and Rachel hadn't even gone out for coffee yet, much less on a proper date. Consequently, asking her to attend something as extravagant as his sister's tenth anniversary celebration seemed like rather a big deal.

But he also knew that if he didn't ask Rachel to go with him to this event, then his sister would instantly pressure him to ask Gloria. And that would only be the beginning of what Myra hoped would be a wonderful relationship. He also knew that Myra was definitely not above guilting him into asking her friend out.

Not only that, but he could see himself faced with having to attend dinners with this Gloria woman at Myra's house. Most likely on a regular basis.

Wyatt could feel the noose tightening around his neck.

Wyatt actually had nothing against his sister's friend, but by the same token he also had nothing *for* her, either. Moreover, he really hated being forced into things or having his arm twisted.

Try as he might, there just didn't seem to be a gracious way out of this disconcerting dilemma. Wyatt's brow furrowed as he tried to find a solution that didn't hurt anyone's feelings.

There didn't seem to be one.

"You're being awfully quiet," George observed as he continued to go through his by now well-rehearsed exercise routine. "I know that it's not like you're Chatty Cathy or anything, but you do talk on occasion. I've heard you," he said with a chuckle.

Snapping out of his mental reverie, Wyatt

eyed his patient. He was not familiar with the term the man had just used.

"Chatty Cathy?" he repeated.

George smiled, remembering. "That was a doll little girls played with years ago. You pulled a string and the doll would talk in a high-pitched voice. Usually saying something either annoying or pretty irritating. I don't think that the doll lasted all that long on the market."

"And I remind you of an annoying doll?" Wyatt asked, trying to make sense out of what his patient had just said to him.

"No, but she did talk a lot and so did you—on occasion. To be honest," George went on, shifting sides as he began a second set of exercises, "I rather like the sound of your voice. It's deep and resonant. And it made me feel like we were sharing a moment."

He was doing his best to try to get the young man to relax and talk, feeling that it was for the best if he could get Wyatt to respond to his efforts.

George paused for a moment, then resumed his attempts to coax information out of the physical therapist.

"Anything on your mind that you want to talk about?" the restaurateur asked Wyatt as casually as he could.

"Just that you've really made a lot of progress now that you've set your mind to it."

He wasn't buying it. George paused and looked at Wyatt pointedly. "I had a heart attack, Wyatt. I did not hit my head. I can tell when someone's trying to pull the wool over my eyes." He continued looking at the young man, waiting.

Cornered, Wyatt assured his patient, "It's nothing I can't handle. Now that you're doing better, let's see about getting you to move on to more difficult exercises."

In response, George groaned, but the sound had more to do with that fact that Wyatt was shutting him out than it did with being given new exercises to undertake and master.

Thirty minutes later, as the session was winding down, George delicately inquired if Wyatt had another patient, or if perhaps he was free for the next half hour or so.

"I've got about an hour before my next patient. Why?" Wyatt asked. "Do you want to extend your session?"

George looked at him, stunned. "What? Oh, Lord, no. What you've got me doing now is more than enough. If I did even a couple more minutes of this, I might just fold up and expire," Rachel's father said with feeling. "I was just asking what your agenda was like because if you're free, maybe you'd like to drop me off at the restaurant so I could get down to some real work."

He saw a skeptical look pass over Wyatt's face. Because he had made such a big deal out of regaining his independence, George knew he had to come up with a plausible excuse to explain his supposed change of heart. So he told Wyatt, "My car's been acting up and if I'm in a vehicle that suddenly dies, I am positive that Rachel will use that as an excuse to ground me." Because the dubious expression on the physical therapist's face was still there, George quickly added, "I can call a mechanic to look my car over while I'm at work."

"That's a pretty specialized ask you're making," Wyatt marveled as he indicated that George should continue with his routine.

"My mechanic and I have known each other for a very long time," George told the therapist, keeping his voice sincere and hoping that the man was buying this. "And the man loves my lasagna. I know for a fact that he would do anything for it," he added proudly.

Wyatt nodded as he watched George continue with his exercises. In his estimation, the man was definitely losing steam. "Sure, I can drop you off," he said.

Busy observing his patient's form, Wyatt missed the grin that came over George's face.

Always on the alert, George was doing everything he could think of to throw his daughter and his physical therapist together as often as was humanly possible. He had witnessed the spark between the two firsthand and he felt that all he had to do was be patient and keep pushing the two of them together until the light dawned on them and they finally realized what they had going between them.

When it came to doing something like that, George prided himself on having infinite patience.

Initially intrigued when Maizie had recommended Wyatt for the dual position of his physical therapist as well as his future son-in-law, George was now completely convinced that the woman had made the right choice. The young man struck him as hardworking, dedicated and the absolute perfect pick for his daughter.

Even being physically drained this way by Wyatt was definitely worth it.

Johanna happened to be walking by the restaurant's front window that looked out on the parking lot. What she saw made her stop in her tracks.

And then she smiled.

Turning back toward Rachel, the assistant manager made her way over to the reservation desk. By the time she stopped in front of it—and Rachel—her radiant smile had gone from ear to ear.

"What?" Rachel asked, knowing that the woman was waiting to be coaxed.

"Well, it looks like your father has gotten himself a new chauffeur," she said.

Rachel glanced at her watch. Again. She'd been doing it now every several minutes for the last hour. She'd expected her father to come in to work much earlier, and had started to worry that maybe something had gone wrong, either with the exercises or with her father.

In order not to let her imagination run away with her and to prevent herself from making noises like an annoying, paranoid daughter, she had thrown herself into overseeing the one hundred and one details involved in running a restaurant.

Preoccupied as she was, it took her a moment to process what the assistant manager was telling her. Putting aside her projections, Rachel quickly moved toward the front of the restaurant.

If he had a chauffeur, that meant her father was at least here. What had taken him so long? she couldn't help wondering. And why was Johanna grinning? It didn't make any sense.

"What are you talking about?" Rachel asked, struggling to keep the irritation out of her voice.

Rachel was torn between the anticipation that the woman had caught a glimpse of her father with Wyatt, and concern that her father was being brought over by an ambulance driver on the way to the hospital.

Ever since that awful, awful accident—it had taken her three days for her own heart rate to slow down—every time there was anything out of the ordinary concerning her father, she was thrown back to that night.

The memory was always accompanied by her breaking out in a cold sweat.

When Rachel made out Wyatt's car, she breathed a huge sigh of relief. "You could have told me that it was Wyatt."

Johanna came up behind her. "I'm sorry," she apologized honestly. "I thought you already knew. You are kind of anal when it comes to watching out for your dad."

Rachel closed her eyes for a moment, gathering herself together. Much as she hated to admit it, Johanna was right. She did have a habit of overreacting when it came to anything to do with her father.

It was going to take her some time to get over that, she thought.

Maybe a hundred years—or so.

Rachel threw open the front door before her father and Wyatt had a chance to enter. "Everything all right?" she asked, her eyes darting from her father to Wyatt and then back again.

Perplexed, her father asked, "Of course. Why shouldn't it be?"

She made eye contact with Wyatt, nodding a greeting at him. The man probably thought she was being neurotic, but well, that boat had already sailed.

"Well, you usually insist on driving yourself in," Rachel reminded him.

"I decided it might be a nice thing to have some company for a change," her father told her. The expression on his face was one of sheer innocence.

Wyatt decided to speak up, stepping between the man and his daughter. "Your father said that his car was acting up and he didn't want to take a chance on getting stuck on the road, so he asked if I could drop him off at the restaurant."

"That sounds like a very smart way for you to think," she commented.

Suspicions began to prick at her as she looked at her father. This didn't sound like him. The man usually threw caution to the wind and opted to take his chances. Her father was the type who leaped long before he even *thought* of looking.

Something else was going on here, she would bet anything on it.

But he was here, in one piece, and he had brought Wyatt with him, so she didn't really feel as if she could find fault with her father.

Taking a deep breath, she said, "Since you've obviously exceeded your quota of good deeds for today and brought him here, the least I can do is offer you some coffee or some dessert. Or both." She gave him a wide, inviting smile.

Wyatt shook his head. "No, that's all right," he began to demur.

But Rachel was not through with her pitch. "We have a fresh batch of cannoli just filled with our special ricotta mixture that comes with chocolate bits and powdered sugar." She looked at his face, searching for some sort of indication that she had gotten to him.

"One bite and you'll think you've gone to heaven," George assured his physical therapist.

Wyatt seemed clearly torn. A second later, his sweet tooth waved a white flag. "Well, maybe just one piece."

"Attaboy. Johanna, get this wonderful young man his first serving of heaven," George instructed his longtime friend. And then he turned toward his daughter, "You look tired, Rachel. Why don't you sit down and keep Wyatt company while Johanna and I get the cannoli?" he suggested.

George didn't wait for his daughter to answer him. Instead, he went off with the assistant manager to get the dessert.

Wyatt nodded, taking a seat at the small table. "I guess I had better do as your dad suggested."

She wasn't sure if her father had twisted Wyatt's arm to get him to stay. "Look, if you're in a hurry, you don't have to stay. You can sneak out now if you need to get going," Rachel told him, indicating the clear path open to his escape.

But Wyatt made no effort to leave. "It wouldn't seem right. The idea of feeding me apparently gives your dad a lot of pleasure," Wyatt said with a laugh. "Besides," he continued, working his way into the topic that was uppermost in his mind, "it'll give me a chance to talk to you."

Alarms went off in her head.

Now what? she wondered.

The next moment, Rachel was upbraiding herself. She really needed to get a handle on letting fear take over.

But she knew very well that doing so was going to take her time.

A lot of time.

"Sure," she replied, taking the seat opposite Wyatt and trying not to look as if she was waiting to be shot out of a cannon. "Should I be bracing myself?"

"Well," he told her thoughtfully, "I suppose that all depends."

"Depends on what?"

"On how you would react to being asked to attend my sister's anniversary party," he told her, his eyes never leaving her face.

That definitely was not what she was expecting him to say. Wyatt's question had managed to catch her completely off guard. "Excuse me?"

For a moment, Wyatt debated making up an excuse and just abandoning the whole thing. But the truth of it was, he did want to go out with her. This seemed to be the perfect excuse for that to happen, so, taking a deep breath he plowed ahead.

"I don't want you to feel as if I'm backing you up against the wall, but you would be doing me a great favor if you said yes." Then he quickly backtracked. "If you can't come, I will totally understand." Still, he didn't want to lose her, either, so he added, "But you need to know that my sister is determined to fix me up with one of her friends and I am going to possibly be trapped in what would amount to a loveless marriage on my part because my sister is not the type of person to *ever* take no for an answer—on anything."

Wyatt looked so terribly serious—and the subject seemed so absurd—she found herself beginning to laugh. Once she did, she almost couldn't stop. Although kindhearted, Wyatt did not strike her as the type to be forced to do anything he didn't want to. He was a man who was in charge of his own destiny.

In a way, that was sort of like her, Rachel couldn't help thinking.

"When is it?" she asked.

"Saturday," he replied, never taking his eyes off her face.

Part of him couldn't help thinking that he had pushed this too far, too soon. But the words were out, so there was nothing he could do about that.

Rachel started to think the situation over. There was no question that she welcomed the chance to spend some time with him, especially using his sister's celebration as an excuse. If she was going to make it, she would have to switch a few things around. Mainly that meant studying.

But the idea of going out with Wyatt—going *anywhere* with Wyatt—caused a smile to rise to her lips.

"Okay," she told him, her eyes meeting his. "I can do it."

Chapter Ten

For just a second, Wyatt was sure that his ears were playing tricks on him and he had just imagined her response.

But the smile on her lips totally sold it.

"That's great," he said enthusiastically. But then another thought occurred to him. "I'm not inconveniencing you by asking you to attend, am I?"

"Why? Is there something else I'm supposed to do besides show up?" Rachel asked. There was more than a hint of amusement in her voice as she looked at him.

"No, nothing else," he told her quickly. And then he thought of his mother. He just prayed she wouldn't start firing questions at Rachel. "And that's plenty, believe me." Wyatt fell back on details. "It starts at six. I can pick you up at five thirty—or any time after that if you'd prefer. It's all up to you."

"Well," Rachel said, pretending to consider his suggestion, "I prefer showing up on time. I'm not the type who enjoys making an entrance."

Rachel might not enjoy it, Wyatt thought, but she was certainly the type who could easily make an entrance without so much as trying.

"Speaking of which," Rachel continued, "is this celebration going to be formal?"

She needed to know what to wear. The worst thing in the world would be to show up dressed too formally or too casually. She didn't want the first impression she made on his family to be a bad one.

What makes you think that even matters? You're probably never going to see any of these people again, she told herself. Still, she didn't want her appearance to somehow reflect badly on Wyatt.

Wyatt answered her question. "I'd say comfortably formal."

"I have no idea what that means."

Realizing he had been obscure, he tried again. "It means wear something nice that won't outshine my sister. Myra's not vain, but this is a pretty big deal to her. In this case it means that she'd like to be the center of attention." He laughed. "How about this? It's being held at the Starlight Room in the Bedford Hotel. Does that help you any?"

She laughed, shaking her head. "What would have helped is if I hadn't asked the question to begin with."

And then she thought of some of her mother's things that her father had saved, leaving the items in her side of their closet.

He hadn't been able to make himself part with any of her mother's favorite outfits. If she remembered, there were some pretty nice things for her to choose from.

"Don't worry, I'll go with my instincts and figure something out." Rachel glanced over at her father, who was in the kitchen, tying on his favorite apron. It was a worn item that her mother had gifted him many years ago. I'm in Charge Here was stitched in blue across the front. She could still remember her mother sitting there, carefully sewing the words.

"How about my father?" she asked Wyatt.

The question came out of nowhere and caught him by surprise. He cleared his throat. "I'm sure I can get my sister to find a place for him at the celebration, although I'm not sure that he'd enjoy sitting with a bunch of people he doesn't know." He smiled. "Eating food that he hadn't prepared… What?" he asked, seeing the amused expression on Rachel's face.

She grinned. "Wow, did you ever overthink that one! I was just asking you how my father was doing with his exercises." Rachel realized her mistake. "I guess I should have made it clear that I was switching topics."

"Yes," he agreed.

"All right, now that you know what I'm talking about, how is my dad doing? Honestly," Rachel stressed before he began to answer. She knew that if she had asked the same question of her father, she would have been given nothing short of a glowing report.

"Honestly," Wyatt said, "he's doing much better than I first expected. Actually, I think that coming back here and feeling as if he's making a meaningful contribution to running the restaurant he loves is playing a huge part in his recovery."

Rachel wasn't about to argue with that. She believed in owning her errors in judgment. "I guess you were right."

"It has nothing to do with being right or wrong," Wyatt said. "It has to do with getting to know what makes a person react a certain way."

She wasn't about to have him brush the accomplishment aside. "Still, you called it and I for one am very happy to see him getting back to being his old self, even if he is bossy," Rachel said. "Thank you."

"Well, you deserve as much credit as I do."

Her brow furrowed. "I don't follow," she confessed. She had no part in making her father do his exercises, which was all Wyatt's domain.

"It's your unfailing support that has your father pushing himself to the next level even when a lot of people in his place would have done the minimal amount—or just given up altogether," he stated flatly. "Don't make the mistake of thinking otherwise."

Flustered, Rachel didn't know what to say in response, so she just murmured, "Thank you," then said something about her having to get back to work because the restaurant was going to be opening in another twenty minutes.

Wyatt nodded. "I understand," he told her, then smiled. "So it's a date?"

A date.

The words sent a ripple all through her, beginning in the center of her stomach.

A date.

She was going on a date.

After all this time, she certainly hoped that she remembered how to act. It had been a long time since she had actually been on a real date.

The thought both excited her and scared her at the same time.

She could feel the tips of her fingers growing icy.

"Rachel?" she heard Wyatt ask. He was looking at her quizzically.

"Yes." The word came out a little louder than she had intended.

Clearing her throat, she gave it a second try. "Yes," she repeated at a more normal level. "It's a date." And then she smiled, her eyes sparkling just a little more as she repeated the words. "It's a date." Her smile grew even wider. "I guess I don't have to give you my address."

Wyatt's smile mirrored hers as their eyes met. "I guess not."

Turning, Rachel murmured her excuse again as she hurried off to the kitchen to check on everything—as well as on her father. The man deserved a hug, she thought, not just for everything he had been through, but for being her father and being alive.

She knew that this news was going to make him happy. He had been carrying far too much guilt, feeling that she had put her life on hold because of him.

How on earth am I going to make it to Saturday, Rachel couldn't help wondering.

She hadn't a clue.

Seeing her father, she walked a little faster. "I've got some news, Dad."

The minutes just dragged, but on the other hand, the hours seemed to fly by. If she was actually going to this celebration with Wyatt, there were dozens of details demanding her attention. That didn't even begin to include the five online lessons she needed to get to. Those were a challenge all their own.

Every time she felt she could stop to take a breather, something else would pop up.

Was it her imagination or had things gotten far more complicated in the last week? It certainly felt that way. She would have loved to take just a little time off to pamper herself in preparation for the upcoming anniversary celebration. She had a feeling that far from being pampered, she would be lucky to simply get dressed for this thing.

Johanna had been observing her and had held her tongue for as long as she could.

"You know, you don't have to work yourself into a frazzle just to make up for the fact that you're going to be out on Saturday afternoon," she told Rachel.

"I know that," Rachel said, hardly looking up. "And for your information, the event doesn't begin until six o'clock. I don't have to leave here until five. Maybe even five fifteen."

Johanna rolled her eyes. "Yeah, you do."

She'd been moving ever since she had gotten in—early—this morning and her temper was a little frayed by now. "Johanna, I am still running Vesuvius and I know when to leave."

"No, you're not, and no, you don't," the assistant manager responded decisively.

What was Johanna talking about? Rachel wondered. It wasn't as if the woman didn't know the situation as well as she did.

She opened her mouth, ready to take Johanna to task, but she never got the chance.

"Your father already told me that he is going to take over running the restaurant until we close up for the night, so you might as well save your breath," Johanna said.

Rachel had no intention of loading her father down with responsibilities. That would be a tremendous step backward for him. Who knew what sort of dangerous consequences that could have on the man?

"You and I both know that my father can't—" Rachel began to protest, trying to appeal to Johanna's common sense.

"Oh, but he can," Johanna maintained, cutting in. "He proudly told me that he was given the go-ahead by the hunk who is taking you out on your first date since that jerk ex of yours walked out on the best thing that ever happened to him."

Rachel didn't want to talk about Elliott. The man was in her rearview mirror. He was history, and he would remain that way.

She pressed her lips together, doing her best to hold on to her temper. After all, she knew that Johanna only meant well.

"This isn't about Elliott..." Rachel began, only to be shut down quickly.

"Isn't it?" Johanna asked knowingly.

She wasn't sure if she could take much more of this. "*What* are you talking about?" Rachel demanded.

"You know very well what I'm talking about, Rachel," Johanna said, her voice softening.

Johanna knew what it meant to live with insecurities. When her husband had been killed overseas, she'd had to fight her own way back to rejoin the living.

"You thought your life was perfectly plotted, and then, through no fault of your own, it just fell off the edge of the earth. Moreover, you found that Elliott wasn't there for you to lean on."

Johanna frowned when she thought of the man Rachel had planned to spend her life with.

"But that does *not* mean that it's going to

happen again." She smiled, thinking of Wyatt. "Given what Mr. Terrific is like, I'll bet you every penny in my banking account that it definitely *isn't* going to happen again. Now," she continued, taking the utensil out of Rachel's hand, "put that spatula down, go home and start getting ready or I'm going to take you over my knee and make you realize that you're acting just like a petulant little girl."

Rachel had absolutely no idea what one had to do with the other, but she had no intention of being bullied like this. "Johanna—"

Johanna leveled a piercing gaze at the younger woman. "Rachel..." The woman's voice trailed off significantly, letting Rachel know that she wasn't about to let her win this argument.

Rachel sighed and threw up her arms. "I don't have time to argue."

"That's right, you don't," Johanna agreed. Out of nowhere, she produced Rachel's shoulder bag and slipped the strap onto her shoulder. "Now go home," she ordered. "Remember, you don't want to upset your father, now, do you?"

"The only one who's going to upset my dad is you if he hears you lecturing me," Rachel pointed out.

"Oh, I don't think so," Johanna told her. "The idea of you actually going out and having a good time is something that is bound to make him very happy." She lowered her voice, a kindly note entering into it. "The fact that you gave up so much for him in order to keep his life running on an even keel has made him feel very guilty."

"But he has nothing to feel guilty about," Rachel argued. "I wanted to do that."

Her hands on Rachel's shoulders, Johanna guided her toward the front door.

"Be that as it may, that has no bearing on this. It still made him feel guilty and your father desperately wants to do something to negate that feeling and to begin to pay you back in some small way for everything you've done for him and given up for him."

Rachel found that digging in didn't keep Johanna from pushing her further toward the door. "Then he should listen to me and stop trying to make me turn into some kind of social butterfly."

Johanna shook her head. "He's your father. You should know that's not going to happen. In his mind, he's done enough listening to you to last a lifetime. It's time for things to return back to normal. Now stop arguing with me and just give in. You know you're not going to have any peace until you do."

Glancing at her watch, Johanna frowned.

"You've just wasted ten precious minutes arguing with me. Now go, find something pretty in your mom's closet to wear and be Cinderella for both of us."

Rachel looked at her. How did Johanna know she was going to wear one of her mother's outfits? Was she that predictable? Even so, she tried to stand her ground, at least for a moment.

"Why didn't you ever follow your own advice?" she asked.

"That's simple," Johanna answered, drawing her closer to the front door. "Because I'm happy here." Lowering both of her hands so that they were now against Rachel's back, she gave it a light push and said, "Now go." She turned toward the young woman who was standing to the side. "Wanda, open the door, please. Rachel here is in a hurry to go home and we don't want her just dashing right through the door to get out."

Wanda, a short young woman with curly, dark hair, appeared slightly doubtful about the whole matter, but she hurried over to comply and open the door anyway. She had no intentions of getting embroiled in an argument.

"Now get going," Johanna instructed, giving Rachel a piercing look. "And be sure to tell me everything on Monday."

That stopped Rachel short. "Monday?" she repeated quizzically. "Just how long do you think this celebration is going to last?"

"I have no idea, but I've got my fingers crossed," Johanna told her. "Now stop talking and start walking. Have I made myself clear?"

Rachel sighed again. She really didn't want to stand around here any longer, arguing with the woman. The thought of actually going out on a date was creating giant ripples of nervousness in her stomach. She did her best to keep them under control.

"Okay, okay," she cried. "Look, I'm going."

Johanna rolled her eyes, looking heavenward. "Thank goodness!" But despite her declaration, the woman made no move to retreat, or step back inside. She looked at Rachel expectantly. "Just so you know, I'm going to keep on standing right here until I hear your car start up."

Rachel tried to look disgruntled. "This is harassment."

"Yes, I know, but I forgive you," she said acting as if she was the one being harassed. "Now go!"

Rachel shook her head and laughed. Johanna was in a class all her own, she thought. And then she did as the woman said and hurried into the parking lot.

Chapter Eleven

Rachel had never given much thought to the fact that she was now the same size that her mother had been at her age, right down to their weight and curves. She was built just the same way her mother had been—except for the fact that she was two inches taller than her mother. Because of that, the clothes were shorter on her, Rachel noted as she slipped on yet another dress.

What might have appeared demure on her mother looked somewhat sexy on her, she thought as she regarded herself from several angles in the wardrobe mirror.

The dress she had just put on was a mint green

halter-top outfit with sparkles that made it appear as if stardust had been dusted all over the material, which clung to her body. It also brought out the green in her eyes.

Maybe this was a little too sexy for the anniversary celebration, Rachel thought. The dress, she knew, would have easily come down to cover her mother's knees.

She paused, studying her reflection.

"Okay, Rach, bottom line. Do you like it and does it make you feel pretty?" she asked the image in the mirror out loud.

The answer to both questions was yes—so why did she feel so nervous about wearing this dress?

"Because you've forgotten what it's like to go out with a guy who makes your heart do flip-flops," she murmured.

Rachel glanced at the pile of dresses she had tried on and then discarded. Maybe she would be better off wearing a somewhat more subdued dress. But while she was debating, she heard the doorbell ring.

Well, that certainly negated any second thoughts she was entertaining. She couldn't very well come down in her robe as if she wasn't ready. He'd think she was like every other woman he might have dated—and she wanted to be special.

After grabbing her small silver purse, Rachel hurried down the stairs.

She managed to reach the door just as Wyatt rang the doorbell for a second time. She pulled it open before the physical therapist had a chance to lift his finger off the button.

"Hi. You're right on time," she said, trying not to make it sound as if she would have actually preferred to have a few more minutes in order to make her final selection.

Oh, who was she kidding? She'd made her choice the moment she had slipped the mint vision on her body. His arrival had just spared her the anguish of further debating the decision with herself.

Wyatt had intended to say something clever in response to her greeting, but what wound up coming out of his mouth was, "And you're absolutely stunning," uttered with deep appreciation as his eyes swept over every inch of Rachel, his smile growing wider with every passing second.

Rachel could feel her cheeks warm. She hoped he didn't notice the change in color. "You don't think it's too much?" she asked.

Wyatt's smile had filtered into his eyes. "If anything, it's too little," he said. The next moment, he realized that she might think that he was being critical and he quickly interjected not an apology exactly, but a retraction. "I'm kidding," he told her, then repeated the phrase a second time for emphasis. "I'm kidding. You look fantastic. My sister may never speak to me again."

She definitely didn't want to cause any problems. "You want me to go change?" she offered, already beginning to turn toward the stairs.

Wyatt was familiar with what could happen if a woman said she was going to go change her outfit. Indecision could very well make the process hours longer.

"Absolutely not," he answered. "You really do look terrific and I don't want you changing a thing about this outfit. I was just kidding about Myra. She's not that insecure."

She wasn't as sure as he was about his sister's confidence. Insecurity about appearance haunted every woman she knew to a greater or lesser degree. But Rachel had no idea what to put on as the runner-up to this dress, The moment she had slipped on this dress, she had known that it was the "one"—even though her doubts had wound up kicking in shortly thereafter.

After a moment, Rachel reluctantly nodded, ending the debate.

"So are we good to go?" Wyatt asked, indicating that if she raised any objections, he was willing to listen to them.

Maybe that was why she was ready to leave for the celebration, because Wyatt seemed so willing to indulge her.

"Yes," Rachel answered with a smile, "I'm all set."

He became aware of her bare shoulders. "Do you have a shawl or anything like that to wear?" he asked, looking around the room to see if she had laid anything out. "The temperature is supposed to drop tonight. I don't want you to catch a cold because you're doing me a good turn."

Wow, talk about thinking ahead! Rachel was impressed by his thoughtfulness.

"As a matter of fact," she said, walking over to the coat closet by the front door, "I do." She took a shawl out of the closet, draped it over her arm and rejoined him.

"Once more with feeling," she declared, tilting her head up so that she could look into his eyes. She felt a warm shiver work its way up and down her spine, doing a much better job of warming her than any shawl ever could.

Wyatt could have sworn he felt her smile working its way into his system. Within seconds, it succeeded in taking him prisoner.

"My thoughts exactly," he murmured belatedly. Opening the front door, he held it for her, waiting for Rachel to walk out of the house.

"Are you sure your sister won't mind my coming to this on such short notice?" she asked. Important anniversary parties that were also milestones were meant to be celebrated with family and friends, not strangers who happened to tag along.

"Mind?" he asked incredulously. "Myra's been consumed with curiosity ever since I told her I had someone to bring with me."

He stood aside as she locked and secured the front door.

"She wanted to fix you up with one of her friends if I remember correctly," Rachel recalled. He held the car door open for her and once again she had to silently admit that he had impressive manners. "Won't she hold that against me?" she asked, sliding in.

"My sister might have some bad moments on occasion," Wyatt admitted as he got in on his side, "but by and large Myra's got a good heart and she genuinely wants everyone to be happy, including me. What did you say earlier in the week about overthinking things?" he asked, pointedly glancing at her before he backed out of the parking space.

"Point taken," Rachel allowed. "By the way," she went on, "I wanted to get your sister and her husband something but since I don't know either of them and don't have a clue what they might or might not like, I decided to just get a gift certificate for them."

Wyatt couldn't help appreciating her thoughtfulness. He hadn't expected Rachel to give his sister and her husband anything. He had been too busy feeling triumphant about getting her to agree to be his date.

"Myra's really going to love you," he predicted, flashing a smile at Rachel.

"It's just a gift certificate," Rachel protested, brushing off his compliment. After all, it wasn't *that* big an amount, although it definitely wasn't that small, either.

"It's the thought that counts," Wyatt reminded her. "And besides, my sister *loves* spending money. I guarantee you have just gone to the top of her list even though she doesn't know you—yet. But that's probably going to change by the end of the evening." He could see her stiffening her shoulders out of the corner of his eye. "This is going to be painless." he promised her. "Except for possibly my mother."

That phrase instantly caught Rachel's attention. "Oh?"

He heard the wariness in her voice. "Don't worry about it," Wyatt told her. "My mother likes to be critical of everything. My career path, my sister's choice of a husband, the way my father dresses. The way to make my mother happy is to provide her with something to complain about. If she didn't have anything to criticize, I guarantee that she would be absolutely miserable. So, if you give her something to disapprove of, you actually contribute to my mother's happiness."

She shook her head, attempting to absorb all this in and sort it out.

"You have a very complicated family, Wyatt," Rachel told him. She drew her purse in closer to her for comfort and to reassure herself that she still had the couple's gift with her.

Wyatt laughed at her comment. She had hit the situation right on the head. "Tell me about it."

Trying to distract herself, Rachel decided to ask Wyatt a few questions about his sister that might help her get through the evening.

"So tell me, what's your sister like?"

"In a word, bossy." He grinned. "But that's just my point of view. She's also very sweet and outgoing—and perpetually trying to lose five pounds," he added, "even though Matthew is forever telling her that she's perfect just the way she is."

Matthew. That would be Myra's husband, Rachel thought. She smiled at what Wyatt had said. "He sounds very nice."

"He is," he told her with feeling. "To have lasted fifteen years with my mother pecking away at him like some sort of invading rooster, I'd say that he damn well has to be."

"Fifteen years?" Rachel echoed quizzically. "I thought you said this was their tenth anniversary." Had she gotten that part wrong?

"Oh, it is," he answered. "But they dated for five years first. My mother kept trying to get Myra to see other guys, saying that she felt Myra needed to experience more of life so she could be sure before she 'jumped into the marriage' and sealed her fate." His mouth curved. "As you can see, my mother's a hopeless romantic."

"I don't understand," Rachel confessed. "If your mother feels that way, why is she even coming to this anniversary celebration?"

Wyatt laughed. "That," he told her, "is part of the mind-boggling mystery that is my mother. And like I said, my mother's not happy unless she had something to complain about. My sister's marriage provides her with more than ample opportunity—even though she had to couch her reaction in subtle language."

Rachel shook her head as she drew in a deep breath. "I can see that this is going to be a lot of fun," she quietly predicted.

Wyatt spared her a glance and grinned before he looked back at the road. She was beginning to get the hang of it, he thought.

"You know, if you had told me this beforehand, I might have given you a different answer when you asked me to go with you."

"I know," Wyatt acknowledged, "but I really wanted you to come with me as my date."

Rachel stared at his profile for a long moment. She had the impression that Wyatt meant what he had just said. She had no idea why that made her as happy as it did—but it really did.

Wyatt pulled up his car into the hotel's parking lot less than ten minutes later. Turning off the engine, he looked at her.

"Want a few minutes to pull yourself together?" he offered.

"Nope," she answered. "If I take those few minutes, I might just decide to turn around and walk home."

"You do realize that you're talking about fifteen miles?" he asked.

She looked unfazed. "However long it takes."

Then, taking in a deep breath, she exhaled, opened her door and swung her legs out.

Realizing that she was about to get out of the car and not entirely sure what she was going to do after that, Wyatt quickly got out on his side and hurried over to hers.

Taking her arm, he carefully escorted her out of the vehicle.

Rachel looked at him, amused. “I am perfectly capable of getting out of your car on my own.”

“I know,” Wyatt answered cheerfully. “I just wanted to do it right—and maybe also to keep you from escaping.” He gave her a wide grin. “You did say you were contemplating walking home.”

“I was kidding,” she told him. There was no way she would walk home from here, not after having put in more than half a day’s work at the restaurant. She didn’t have *that* much energy left at her disposal. She’d said that when she had been momentarily annoyed.

“Maybe you were,” he acknowledged, “but I don’t know you well enough to know that for certain.”

There was a twinkle in her eye as she looked at him. She was beginning to relax a little. “I guess you don’t at that,” she admitted. “But for future reference, I really don't hike all that well when I'm in high heels."

She turned her attention to the hotel they were entering. She'd seen the Bedford Hotel countless times as she'd driven by it, but she had never had an occasion to actually enter the building. She found it inviting. Its decor was very pleasing to the eye.

Despite never having been here before, she felt instantly at home.

"This seems like a nice place," she commented to Wyatt as they walked inside.

"It is," Wyatt agreed. And then he went on to tell her, "Matthew always likes to say, 'Nothing but the best for my wife.' The thing about it is that he genuinely means it."

The more she heard about Wyatt's brother-in-law, the more she found herself liking the man. She couldn't begin to understand why Wyatt's mother found fault with her son-in-law. In her place, she would have been overjoyed that her daughter had found someone so thoughtful and loving.

"That really sounds nice. What does your mother have against him?"

"Depends on what day of the week you ask," Wyatt told her with a laugh. "But between you and me, I think that deep down she knows that

Myra made the right choice, even though she did it without consulting my mother. My mother just can't admit it without feeling as if she is losing face."

He guided her down the hallway. The Starlight Room was at the very end of it. The sign right beside the door said Reserved for a Private Party. Wyatt paused to look at Rachel. "Ready?"

No, she wasn't, but she wasn't going to get any readier just standing here. "Just open the door."

Wyatt pretended to take a little bow. "Your wish is my command," he replied glibly, pushing the door open for her.

The wall of noise hit her immediately. Rachel looked around and saw that the entire room was packed. She could easily get lost in the crowd.

Maybe it wouldn't be so bad after all.

With that, she slipped her arm through Wyatt's and entered the ballroom, telling herself that she wasn't nervous.

Chapter Twelve

It took exactly ninety seconds after Wyatt and Rachel had crossed the threshold into the ballroom for Wyatt's mother to hone in on them.

Once Ariel Watson had spotted her son and the young blonde on his arm, the small, powerful matriarch made a beeline for them.

Her eyes intently focused on her "target," Ariel quickly wove her way around an inordinate amount of couples who were milling around, making small talk while they appeared to be waiting for the festivities to officially begin.

His mother was exceedingly fast for someone her age, Wyatt thought when he saw her heading toward them, moving like shark about to launch into an overdue feeding frenzy.

It was too late to turn around and leave, he feared. His mother would most likely just make a scene. Their only chance was to stand their ground.

He really hoped that Rachel was up to this.

Leaning his head in toward her ear, he warned Rachel, "Brace yourself. Incoming."

Rachel had been busy taking in the general scene around them and didn't immediately grasp what Wyatt was telling her.

Turning toward him, she asked, "What?"

"Mother at three o'clock," he told her, nodding in that general direction.

Wyatt didn't dare point his mother out for Rachel's benefit because he knew the woman would see his gesture. He didn't want to alert his mother even a second before they came together that they'd noticed her coming.

Rachel instantly looked toward the part of the room Wyatt had indicated. She could feel her stomach tightening as she readied herself for the interrogation.

Calm down, Rach. If you can get through your dad's long journey back to his old life, you can get through and put up with anything.

Heartened to some degree, she pasted a wide

smile on her lips. She was not about to let the woman know that she was intimidated by her. If nothing else, she owed this to Wyatt for getting her father back to his old self.

"So," Ariel said on reaching them. Her alert brown eyes took in virtually every single inch of the young woman standing next to her son. "This is her."

"Yes," Rachel answered before Wyatt had a chance to say anything, "this is me." Leaning forward, Rachel extended her hand toward the older woman. "How do you do, Mrs. Watson? Congratulations on your daughter and son-in-law's milestone anniversary."

Ariel made a vaguely dismissive sound as she waved her hand at the words. "Ten is not a milestone. Now, twenty-five or fifty, *those* are milestones."

"Still, ten isn't all that shabby," Rachel told her. "Baby steps," she added with a smile.

Apprehensive that his mother was going to escalate this exchange into a full-blown argument, Wyatt prepared to jump in, ready to draw Rachel out of the line of fire and leave if it came to that.

Instead, his mother surprised him by nodding her head at Rachel's comment. "Baby steps," she repeated as if she agreed with the evaluation.

"So," Ariel continued, leveling a piercing look

at the young woman. Rachel could have sworn the look had gone straight down into her chest. "Just what is it that you do?"

"Mom." There was a warning note in Wyatt's voice, telling his mother to back off. The last thing he wanted was for Rachel to feel as if she was being interrogated. It nothing else, he felt that his mother's manner was insulting.

Ariel turned her head and gave her son an amazingly innocent look. "I'm just curious, Wyatt. Can't a mother be curious about the young woman her son brought to his sister's anniversary celebration?" she asked in an almost childlike manner.

Who did his mother think she was kidding? They both knew that this wasn't curiosity, Wyatt thought. His mother was grilling Rachel and he felt as if he needed to protect her before this got worse.

"It's okay," Rachel told Wyatt complacently, holding up her hand to make him keep back any other accusing words. "I don't mind answering." She turned to his mother. "Right now, I am currently helping to run my father's restaurant—"

"Helping?" Ariel asked, obviously keenly interested in learning every single detail about this young woman's life. "Was your father thinking of retiring?"

"Dad had a heart attack, so I stayed on to help him keep the restaurant going. He truly loves that place," she said without any reservation.

"You stayed on," Ariel parroted as if the phrase somehow felt foreign to her. "Does that mean, before any of this happened, you were planning on going somewhere?"

Rachel nodded. "Yes, ma'am. College."

For once, Wyatt noted, his mother actually looked impressed. But then her confrontational nature reasserted itself. "And where was your mother while all this was going on?"

"Mom!" Wyatt chided, really annoyed now.

But Rachel answered Ariel calmly, "My mother died some years ago."

For once, Ariel was speechless. And then, recovering, she said, "I'm sorry to hear that." Wyatt actually thought it sounded as if his mother meant that. "No siblings to pitch in?" she asked.

Rachel took the question in stride. "I'm afraid that I'm an only child."

"And you gave up college to help your father?" Wyatt's mother asked incredulously, as if trying to absorb the information.

"To be accurate, I postponed it. Actually, right now I am in the process of taking online classes at night and trying not to fall too far behind in my studies," Rachel said.

"Really?" Ariel marveled.

Wyatt was surprised there was no note of sarcasm or cynicism in his mother's voice. Instead, he realized, she actually looked as if she was impressed by what Rachel had just told her.

Quite honestly, he was still waiting for the other shoe to drop. But for the first time in as long as he could remember, Wyatt felt that just might not happen.

"Wyatt, don't just stand there like a statue. Go get this lovely young lady a plate of canapés," his mother instructed.

"No, that's fine, Mrs. Watson, I am perfectly capable of getting my own plate." Rachel smiled at the woman who, she thought, looked rather motherly in her own way. "It's just nice to be out in public for a change instead of working in the restaurant or trying to catch up on my studies. Coming here is kind of a treat for me," she admitted.

Ariel nodded. "If you don't mind my asking," she began.

Wyatt braced himself, ready to jump in and tell his mother to back off if her question got too personal—which it generally did. There was just no letting his guard down around his mother, he thought wearily.

Seeing the look on Wyatt's face, Ariel protested, "I was just going to ask her how the two of you happened to meet. Is that so terrible?"

Rachel saw nothing wrong with that. It gave her the opportunity to talk Wyatt up. She remembered that he had said his mother wasn't happy about his choice of vocation. Maybe this could get her to change her mind, at least a little.

"Before the doctor would clear my father to get back to work—something my father desperately wanted to do—he needed to take some physical therapy sessions—and do well with them. But my father isn't the easiest man to handle. He kept firing all the physical therapists who came to work with him—until," she informed Ariel with a smile, "your son came along.

"Apparently, Wyatt has just the right magic touch," Rachel continued. "My father stopped snapping at his physical therapist and finally *listened* to what was being said. Thanks to your son's efforts, my father is *finally* getting better and stronger." She turned to smile at Wyatt, then addressed Ariel, "You should be very proud of your son."

Ariel pursed her lips together, then shot a look

in Wyatt's direction. "I've been told that," she said to Rachel.

"Well, it's true. My father is a very stubborn man and your son got him to respond in a way that I've never seen him respond. He's actually almost docile." Her smile widened a little more. "He really likes your son."

"Hmm." Ariel allowed herself no further response than that. And then she quietly instructed, "Well, enjoy yourselves tonight. I'm sure I'll be seeing you around, Rachel," she said just before she withdrew from her son and Rachel. She sought out some other people, family members she was not all that crazy about but was willing to tolerate for the space of one evening.

The moment it was safe, Rachel blew out a long breath. She felt oddly calm at this point. "Well, that went better than I thought it would."

When Wyatt didn't respond, she turned to look at him. For his part, Wyatt was staring at her unabashedly. "What?" she asked.

"Why didn't you tell me?" he asked, his expression not changing.

"Tell you what?" Rachel asked. She didn't have a clue what he was talking about. Apparently, tonight was going to require a great deal of patience on her part.

"That you're a sorceress," he said simply.

Rachel blinked. "What?"

"A sorceress," he repeated. "I have *never* seen my mother take to anyone the way she just took to you. She was positively *nice*." He was clearly in awe of what he had just witnessed.

"I didn't do anything special. I just answered her questions," Rachel said with a shrug.

"You did more than that. You cast a spell over her," Wyatt told her. "I have never seen her take an interest in anyone—including me and any of my siblings—the way she just did with you. You have extraordinary powers," Wyatt marveled. "I hope you continue using them for good."

"Maybe the problem is that you let your mother get under your skin and get too defensive when she says anything."

Wyatt shrugged. "Say what you will. But as for me, I'm planning on keeping you around as a good-luck talisman."

She looked at him. The idea of his saying that he wanted to keep her around instantly caused a warm glow to spread all over her. She knew he was just kidding, but it would be really nice if just *part* of him actually meant what he had just said.

C'mon, Rach, you don't have any time to get involved with anyone. Even if this had a chance of working out—and there are absolutely no *guarantees of that—you have a life to catch up on. You had a late start, remember? Don't stall out altogether,* she warned herself. *Just get your head in gear and do what you need to do.*

"Earth to Rachel," Wyatt was saying, looking at her curiously.

When she realized that she had allowed herself to slip away, she looked up into his eyes, contrite.

"Hey, where did you just go?" Wyatt asked her, amused.

"Nowhere," she answered defensively. "I was just thinking that maybe you were being too hard on your mother." Rachel grabbed at the first thing that occurred to her.

"Well, before I witnessed this display tonight, I would have said I was being way too charitable to her," Wyatt laughed. "To be honest, I've heard people refer to my mother as 'you-know-who.' That includes my own father—although not within her hearing range, of course," he admitted, his grin widening. "As far as I'm concerned, I feel as if I just witnessed a Christmas miracle—four months before Christmas."

Rachel smiled at him, pleased at the way everything had gone. "Why don't we go get some canapés like your mother suggested. I suddenly feel very hungry."

He nodded. "I guess practicing witchcraft can really take a lot out of you.

"Ouch!" he cried, stunned as he grabbed hold of his shoulder.

Rachel had caught him totally by surprise. He hadn't expected her to suddenly punch his biceps with her doubled-up fist.

But then, he thought, massaging his arm to get the circulation going, doing the unexpected was entirely in keeping with the woman's behavior.

"Canapés, not a bad idea," he agreed. "People are beginning to line up now."

Taking her over to the line that was forming, Wyatt introduced Rachel to several people that he knew.

And then, belatedly, he saw that his sister and brother-in-law were also in the same line.

"You made it," Myra declared, pleased, as she hugged her brother.

She was looking not at him, but at the woman Wyatt had brought with him. She raised her eyebrow in his direction, silently asking him for an introduction.

"Myra, Matthew, I'd like you to meet Rachel. Rachel here just survived a heavy-duty display of Mom's interrogation talents. She not only survived, she won Mom over."

"You're kidding!" Matthew marveled, looking at Rachel with wonder and admiration in his eyes. "Really? I haven't been able to do that in fifteen years. What's your secret?"

She shook her head. "Your brother-in-law exaggerates," Rachel told him.

But Wyatt waved a hand at Rachel's modesty. "Don't listen to her. I was stunned speechless."

Wanting to draw attention away from what Wyatt was saying, Rachel opened her purse and took out the anniversary card along with the gift certificate she had placed inside it. She held it out to Myra.

"Happy Anniversary," she told the couple. "Wyatt wasn't being very helpful, so I didn't know what you might like as a gift. I thought that I couldn't go wrong with a gift card—unless it was for some obscure place," she conceded. "This one isn't. It can be used anywhere."

Myra and Matthew exchanged looks and Myra's face lit up as she said, "I know just the place where we can use this," she told Rachel. Hugging her brother's companion, Myra said, "Thank you!" with more enthusiasm than Rachel thought the gift warranted.

"You're welcome," Rachel replied, feeling just

a little confused. "If you don't mind my asking, where are you thinking of using this gift card?"

His sister exchanged looks with her husband again. It was obvious that the couple had a secret that they were just bursting to share.

"So," Wyatt said, "Are you going to answer the question, or are you planning on keeping us guessing for the duration of the evening?" He looked pointedly from his sister to his brother-in-law.

To his surprise, Rachel was the one who came to the couple's defense. "It's okay, Wyatt. Don't pressure them. They'll tell us when they're ready to. Right?" she asked, looking at Myra.

His sister smiled at Rachel, then looked at her brother in turn.

"You made the right choice, little brother," she told him. "Smart thinking is a really good quality for an uncle."

"An uncle?" Wyatt questioned. He looked from his sister to Matthew. "Does this mean…?"

"It does," Myra practically squealed. "We're having a baby!"

Chapter Thirteen

A second, louder shriek came on the heels of the first.

There were less than five seconds separating the two. It melded into the noise the crowd was making, but Rachel managed to pinpoint its source and the direction it was coming from.

She quickly tugged on Wyatt's arm to get his attention. Wyatt was just about to hug Myra and looked quizzically in Rachel's direction. He hadn't heard the second squeal.

"I think you'd better get ready to catch your mother," Rachel told him. "She looks like she's about to pass out."

Wyatt thought of his mother as having the constitution of an old warhorse. He was about to contradict Rachel when he glanced in his mother's direction and saw her pale face.

"Oh, wow," he exclaimed, quickly making his way to her. Reaching her just in time, he put his arms around his mother as she was beginning to sink down to the floor.

"Mom? Mom?" Wyatt cried urgently. "It's all right. Open your eyes!"

The words seemed to snap Ariel out of her temporary departure from the immediate world. "All right?" she echoed, looking up at her son as if the words he had just uttered didn't make any sense. "It's downright wonderful!"

Pulling herself together, Wyatt's mother straightened her shoulders and made her way directly over to her daughter, gesturing the guests who were in her path out of her way.

"Myra! Really?" Ariel cried in stunned disbelief. "You're pregnant?"

Myra was pressing her lips together to keep from crying tears of joy. One defiantly slid down her cheek. She nodded, beaming.

"Why didn't you tell me as soon as you found out?" Ariel demanded. She looked accusingly at her daughter. "And what are you doing on your feet? Sit, sit! Someone bring a chair over for my daughter," Ariel ordered.

Several people immediately jumped to drag chairs over.

Wyatt leaned over and whispered into Rachel's ear. "Something tells me that maybe Myra should have kept this a secret a little longer—like maybe until just right before she delivered."

Rachel laughed. "Your sister probably told her now so that your mother wouldn't start criticizing her about all the weight she was gaining in the months that lie ahead."

Wyatt grinned at Rachel as he impulsively hugged her to him. "You're learning, Rachel. You're definitely learning."

"Well," Wyatt overheard his mother say as she glanced over in his direction, "Two down, one to go," Ariel declared pointedly.

Wyatt shook his head. "That woman is never satisfied," he told Rachel, knowing she had to have caught his mother's words, as well.

"Who's the other one 'down'?" Rachel asked him, curious about the reference.

"That would be my brother, Jake. He's the oldest one," Wyatt told her. "He and his wife, Mary, moved to North Dakota. My guess is it was to get away from my mother. They don't have any kids yet. And Mom started nagging them about that. But now that Myra's going to make her a grandmother, maybe Jake and Mary will move back to Southern California. From what I hear, Mary was never crazy about the cold weather."

Rachel looked a little wistful. He raised one eyebrow, silently asking her if anything was wrong.

She was tempted to pretend ignorance, then decided to be honest with Wyatt. She had always valued honesty. "It must be nice having a big family."

"It would be," he agreed, "if my mother wasn't as vocal as she is about everything she views as a disappointment or a shortcoming."

"Someday," Rachel predicted, thinking of her own mother, "a long time from now, you might find that you miss the sound of her voice."

Wyatt shrugged. "It'll have to be a long, long, *long* time from now," he answered. "C'mon, let's finally get something to eat. The line to the canapés table might be clear by now, seeing as how everyone is surrounding my sister and her husband."

Rachel placed her hand in his.

Rachel had to admit that she was having a wonderful time. Between rubbing elbows with

Wyatt and Myra's friends and having several helpings of food, everything felt perfect.

Ordinarily, she never had much of a chance to eat at work. In the last two years she had always been too busy making it to actually eat and enjoy it. And by the time she got home at night, she was too tired to eat. There were always classes to catch up on.

After all the guests at the celebration had had at least one serving of the main meal, if not two, the band began to play. For the most part what they played was happy music with a fast beat.

"Would you like to dance?" Wyatt asked her after two numbers had been played. He looked as if he was ready to get up, assuming that her answer was going to be yes.

But she remained just where she was. "Would you like to have your feet stepped on?"

Wyatt laughed, then pretended to regard her skeptically.

"You can't really be that bad," he told her, ready to draw back her chair.

"I wouldn't be taking any bets on that if I were you."

Wyatt refused to believe her. "You know, I really don't think that you give yourself enough credit, Rachel."

"I'm just issuing you a fair warning," she said.

Wyatt paused, listening to the song that the band was just beginning to play. It was one he was familiar with. "It's a slow number. All you have to do is move your feet a little and sway your hips once in a while. That's not very complicated and everyone will think that you're dancing," he guaranteed. "Besides, the buzz about Myra and her pregnancy hasn't died down yet. That'll take the focus off you. So you can relax."

"I don't think so," Rachel said seriously, still sitting right where she was.

"Oh, c'mon," Wyatt urged. "What do you have to lose?" He was standing next to her chair and holding out his hand, waiting for her to take it.

"My dignity?" It was more of a question than a statement.

He laughed. "Nobody comes to one of these things to show off their dignity, Rachel. Remember, you agreed that this is your day to cut loose and enjoy yourself. Tomorrow it will be back to cleaning the castle, Cinderella. But tonight you get to be the belle of the ball," Wyatt told her.

"Belle of the ball. That role is reserved for your sister," she pointed out.

"Okay," Wyatt agreed amicably. "That means that no one is paying attention to you so you can dance any way you want to." Again, he put out his hand to her.

She frowned, not taking it. But then she conceded, "I'm running out of arguments."

"Good." He grinned. "Because I'm running out of things to say to persuade you." Placing his hands on her shoulders, Wyatt drew her up to her feet. "C'mon," he urged, "can't you hear? They're playing our song."

She listened to the music for a moment. The band had concluded the previous number and was now playing yet another one. It took her a moment to pinpoint the song's title.

"'Sincerely'?" she asked incredulously. Was he serious? "*Our* song is 'Sincerely'?" Rachel repeated, staring at Wyatt.

"Rachel," he replied patiently. "Our song is anything you want it to be as long as I can get you to dance with me. So are you ready to finally yield to me?"

"You are persistent, I'll give you that," Rachel said. For now, she decided to surrender. It was a small point to concede. And she did like this song. It reminded her of her mother, who used to sing it to her when she had been a little girl.

Wyatt laughed under his breath. "It runs in the family," he told her, looking in his mother's direction.

Ariel Watson had clamped down on his sister and it didn't look as if she was about to release her hold on the young woman anytime soon.

Following his glance, Rachel saw that his mother was still talking Myra's ear off, holding on to the young woman's hand and on occasion patting it.

"I kind of feel sorry for your sister," she told Wyatt.

"Don't be. This is a good kind of attention and it beats the prying kind—my mother's usual mode of attention—by a country mile. Right now it looks like she's dedicating herself to my sister's comfort. You know," he went on, looking down into Rachel's upturned face, "that doesn't sound like all that bad of an idea if you ask me." His mouth curved. "Maybe I should do the same thing."

"Dedicate yourself to Myra's comfort?" Rachel asked, amused.

"No," he answered, his voice low and suddenly extremely sexy. "To yours."

Rachel felt it again. Those warm ripples that seemed to undulate sensuously up and down all along her skin, making her particularly aware of every single bone in her body.

Aware of the way his hand felt, holding hers, and the way his body seemed to fit against hers as if they were extensions of one another as they both swayed in time to the music.

"By the way," Wyatt continued, "in case you haven't noticed, you're dancing." His smile widened, filtering into his eyes. "Quite well, I might add."

"Don't compliment me," she quietly requested. "Or you'll make me miss a step."

"Don't worry," Wyatt replied, drawing her even closer against him. "If you miss that step, I'll be sure to find it for you," he promised, whispering the words against her hair.

She shouldn't have come, Rachel thought. Being here with Wyatt like this had managed to create a longing within her that she hadn't experienced in a very long time.

Too long, she realized.

Again, Rachel silently told herself that she didn't have time for this.

Didn't have time to invest in developing any sort of a relationship.

Relationships were for later, once she was satisfied that her father was fully recovered and she was finally finished getting a nursing degree. *Then* she could think about having a relationship.

But somehow, despite the logical sense all of that made, she found herself tempted more and more by that desire.

What had she gotten herself into?

"Are you having a good time?" she heard Wyatt ask her.

It felt as if not only his breath but his words, too, were gliding down along her skin, stirring her. Seducing her.

She knew it was breaking some sort of rule written down in the first-date handbook, but she had never been the one to be coy.

"Yes," she told him, "I am. But then I wouldn't have said yes to coming here with you if I had thought it would be otherwise."

"I'm glad, then," he told her. "Although I have to admit that I had some concerns about you having to put up with my mother. I was afraid that she would have had you running for the hills. She's good at doing that to people."

"I like your mother," Rachel said, surprising him. "I grant you that she's a wee bit unusual, but it's all based totally on love."

That really caught him off guard. "Oh?" Wyatt laughed, drawing her back a little so he could look into her eyes. "And you know this how?"

"From all of my years at the restaurant," she answered seriously. "Observing customers as they interacted with one another. With family members."

He pretended to solemnly consider her words.

"Then I guess I should watch myself around you if I don't want to give anything away."

What she wanted to ask was, *Like what?* But she didn't. Instead she said, "Oh, definitely," trying very hard not to laugh.

"Warning taken under advisement," Wyatt responded. The song had ended and another one, a far livelier one, took its place.

She had expected Wyatt to lead her back to their table.

Instead, he continued dancing with her, holding her in his arms as the tempo increased. His dancing kept pace with the song.

"We're never going back to our table, are we?" Rachel asked him.

"Oh, eventually," he acknowledged. "Right now I am having far too much fun enjoying this new, liberated Rachel."

"Be sure to tell my father that when you carry my limp, unconscious body home tonight. I guarantee he'll be waiting up and he'll want to know what you did to me to get me so exhausted."

"That doesn't worry me." He grinned. "Your father likes me."

Rachel knew he wasn't bragging. She was very aware of just how much her father regarded Wyatt with gratitude and affection. She herself was exceedingly thankful for everything Wyatt had managed to do and accomplish, working with her father.

"He does, doesn't he?" she said by way of agreement. "That really does put you in a class all by yourself. My father doesn't take to many men—or women for that matter." *With the exception of Johanna*, she thought. "I can probably count the whole lot of them on five fingers of one hand. Most of the time he has a personality not unlike that of a wounded lion with a large thorn stuck in his paw."

"Colorful," Wyatt commented. He spun her around one final time as the music wound down.

"On the contrary," Rachel corrected him. "I prefer to think of it as truthful."

The band was playing a slow song now, and without really thinking about it, Rachel found herself resting her head against Wyatt's shoulder as she let herself go with the new tempo.

It just seemed like the thing to do, she thought, letting the moment and the mood lead her.

She caught herself hoping this evening—and most of all, this fantasy that had slipped over her—would never end.

But she knew that there was no getting away from the inevitability that it would.

Still, she was grateful for the time that she had been able to harvest.

Chapter Fourteen

"I guess this is what Cinderella must have felt like when she heard the tower clock strike midnight," Rachel commented.

All the guests in the ballroom had either already left or were in the process of leaving. Rachel realized with some regret that she and Wyatt would have to go, as well.

She jumped slightly as she felt Wyatt slipping her shawl about her shoulders. Focused on the other guests, she hadn't been prepared for that. His hands lingered there for a long moment, doing far more to warm her than the shawl possibly could.

"Well, it's not exactly quite that late," he informed her with a smile, referring to her comment about midnight. "But I promise I won't be turning into a pumpkin."

"That was the coach," Rachel tactfully reminded him. It was a children's story so it was easy to see how he might have gotten his details confused. "The *coach* turned back into a pumpkin, not the prince."

"So I'm the prince?" Wyatt asked, raising an amused eyebrow.

Sometimes she talked too much. Right now, she felt it was safer if she just changed the subject.

She glanced down at the shawl that was wrapped around her shoulders.

"Taking this shawl along was a really good idea," she told Wyatt.

He smiled down into her face as they slowly made their way through the ballroom. "I guess I have my moments."

Yes, he certainly did, Rachel couldn't help thinking. But that wasn't something that she was willing to admit to him out loud. She didn't want Wyatt thinking that she was flirting with him—at least more than she actually was doing.

As they made their way toward the door, Rachel was very aware of him.

Aware of his hand against her back, guiding her through the groups of people saying their goodbyes and congratulating the parents-to-be one last time.

She was also acutely aware of the cologne he was wearing that seemed to wind its way through her whole system.

She supposed that this was the result of her not going out for the last two years, except when she was going to the restaurant and then coming back home to slavishly take those online classes.

But until Wyatt came along, what Elliott had done to her had left a very bad taste in her mouth.

She'd definitely had no desire to socialize with a man on any sort of personal basis. But then Wyatt had changed everything.

However, Rachel knew she couldn't allow herself to get carried away. Once upon a time, Elliott had seemed like the answer to a prayer. At least when they had first started seeing each other.

But as time passed, she'd begun to see flaws in the man.

Very large flaws.

She supposed that she had been willing to turn a blind eye to all those flaws, forgiving him—until she had to remain behind and take care of her father after his heart attack while Elliott continued with his plans to go onto college without so much as even thinking about how abandoned that made her feel.

She frowned, remembering the hurt, although she knew that she couldn't have very well asked him to stay behind. She had sent him off making him feel that he had her blessings.

But then Elliott had never called to find out how her father was doing.

There had been exactly one call from him, and it wasn't even to ask about her father's condition. He had called to say something to the effect of how hard it was settling into a fast-paced college life.

After that, there was nothing.

Not a single word.

She had had to learn from friends that he had found someone else to take her place and that their dating had quickly gotten serious.

And then, shortly thereafter, he had married the young woman. A baby, she found out, came nine months later.

It was an excessively bitter pill for Rachel to swallow.

"Is something wrong?" she heard Wyatt ask as they made their way up to the front of the room and his sister and brother-in-law. "You've gotten exceedingly quiet," he observed.

"No," Rachel quickly retorted. "I was just thinking about what a nice time I've had."

"Well, you don't look like someone who's just had a nice time," Wyatt commented, then, in the next second, he decided to cover for her. "But you're probably just tired. Having fun can take a great deal out of you."

"Maybe," Rachel allowed, thinking how much nicer Wyatt was about things than Elliott had ever been. For one thing, he seemed exceedingly understanding, always placing other people ahead of himself. That was something that she couldn't recall Elliott ever doing.

The next moment, they had reached the head of the line and were saying their goodbyes to Myra and Matthew—and Wyatt's mother.

Amazingly, while the couple looked tired, Ariel Watson did not. The woman looked every bit as fresh as she had when they had first seen her heading straight for them.

"Thank you for coming," Myra said sincerely, embracing Rachel and then her brother.

"Well, thank you for letting me come," Rachel countered.

She looked down at the woman's trim waist. It wouldn't be that way for long. Rachel found herself envying the young woman. She really wanted a baby herself.

Maybe someday, she thought wistfully.

"And if you need anything," Rachel told Wyatt's sister, "please let me know." As she said those words, a thought occurred to her. "And when the time comes, I just want you to know that Vesuvius is a great place to hold a baby shower."

Myra's face lit up. "I will definitely keep that in mind," she promised, barely containing her bubbling excitement.

Ariel seemed to swoop in just at that moment. Her eyes meet Rachel's. "I take it we'll be seeing you again—soon."

"I'd like that," Rachel told the woman with genuine feeling. Her answer seemed to take Ariel completely by surprise.

"I just want you to know that I am planning on holding you to that," Wyatt's mother informed Rachel, pinning her with a penetrating look.

At that point, Wyatt gently guided Rachel out in front of him. "See you, Mom. Dad," he added, nodding at the all but silent, tall man with an incredible amount of snow-white hair, who was standing beside Ariel.

And then, Wyatt managed to get both himself and Rachel out the door without any further verbal exchange with anyone.

The moment they were in the hotel lobby, he turned toward Rachel and said, "You do realize that we're going to have to move, don't you? My mother is not about to forget what you just said about the baby shower."

He had just said "we," Rachel thought. Not that *she* would have to move, but that *they* would have to do it. Was he assuming that they were a couple now?

The thought both excited her as well as frightened her. She honestly didn't know what side she was rooting for.

You're getting carried away again, Rachel chided herself. *This was just a nice evening out, nothing more. You have to remember that.*

"Tell me the truth, did you have a nice time?" Wyatt asked her as he unlocked the car doors with one press of the button on his key fob.

"I had a *wonderful* time," she told him without any reservations as she got into the vehicle.

In the car, Wyatt started it and began driving. Rachel's reaction surprised him. "Even after meeting *you-know-who*?" he asked. They were at a light, which afforded him the opportunity to really look at her.

Laughter entered her eyes as she watched Wyatt studying her closely. The light changed and he was on the move again. She knew he was waiting for an answer.

"Even after that," Rachel replied cheerfully.

Wyatt rolled her words over in his mind and decided that she was being sincere. He liked that about her. Liked the fact that she didn't believe in playing games and was being straightforward.

"She took to you, you know," Wyatt went on. "And that was without her attempting to drag you over the coals. I know you won Matt's total admiration," he told her. "One look at his face could tell you that."

"They make a very nice couple," she said. "I'm really glad that your mother didn't wind up chasing him away."

He nodded. "Well, not that she didn't try, but yeah, they are good for each other."

"And now they're going to be parents," she commented with a wide smile. "Have they been trying for a while?"

"Ever since the honeymoon ten years ago." He thought for a moment. "Possibly before then, but I wouldn't mention that to my mother if I were you," he cautioned.

She turned toward him as he came to a stop at another light. Widening her eyes innocently, she asked him, "Mention what?"

"Attagirl," he said, laughing. "Or should I say 'attawoman'?"

"Labels have never bothered me—unless they're meant to be insults," she told him. She had corrected her father when he referred to her as a girl, but that was another matter entirely.

She could have sworn she saw something flicker across Wyatt's face. Amusement? She wasn't sure.

"I would never insult you," he told her in all seriousness. And then he glanced at the clock on his dashboard. They were getting back to her place later than he had expected. "Think your father might be getting worried?" he asked. "Maybe you should give him a call."

Her lips curved in an amused smile. "I can see why my father likes you so much. Don't worry. We'll be home soon," she told him. "And besides, if I know my dad, he's probably sacked out in front of the TV set, some old rerun playing in the background. He's in his nostalgia period right now, but to be honest, it doesn't matter what's playing. Whatever it is, it's almost guaranteed to put him to sleep.

"My dad is only firing on all four cylinders if he's in the restaurant, presiding over his custom-made stove.

He heard the fondness in her voice. "You two really do get along, don't you?"

"We've been an army of two ever since my mom passed away, so yes, we do. I have to admit that even before he had his heart attack, I was worried about leaving him on his own."

"He's got a full kitchen staff at his beck and call. The man is hardly alone. From what I saw, boss or not, there's a great deal of affection for the man."

"Yes, especially from Johanna," she told him.

"Johanna... That would be the slender older woman who's his assistant manager, right?" he asked.

"You really do pay attention to details, don't you?" she marveled.

"I find that my patients appreciate me taking an interest not just in their disability and their progress, but their lives, as well."

"How long did you say you've been doing this?" she asked him.

"The PT part, a few years. But on my own, for the last six months," he answered.

"Did you just happen to fall into this, or did you always want to have you own physical therapy business?" she asked.

"You want my mother's version, or mine?" he asked Rachel.

"Yours," she answered. "Always yours."

He liked the way that sounded. If his mother didn't somehow manage to scare her away, they could very well have a future together, Wyatt mused.

He liked the way Rachel thought, the way she melded in with his family. He liked *her*.

Really liked her.

It almost stunned him. In all these years, he had never really taken to a woman the way he had to Rachel. She had passed the first hurdle. Meeting his mother hadn't scared her off. With any luck, this might actually go somewhere.

"I always wanted to help people. PT seemed like the way to go," he told her as he drove her home.

The trip was much too short in his opinion. "Well," he said philosophically, "looks like I got you home in one piece."

She grinned as she turned toward him, unbuckling her seat belt.

"Did you think that you wouldn't?" she teased him.

"Actually," he said as he parked his vehicle in her driveway, "I was more worried about the way you'd react meeting my mother."

"Well, I'd say that she and I passed that test

with flying colors," she told him. "Anything else?"

He glanced toward the front of her house. "I still have to walk you to your door and get you inside."

"I'm a big girl. I can get myself inside. But you can definitely walk me to my door if you want to."

His eyes washed over her. There was enough moonlight for him to be able to make out all of her features. He could definitely feel his longing growing.

"Oh, I definitely want to," he confirmed.

Helping her out of his car, Wyatt took hold of her arm and escorted her up to her door, assuming a leisurely pace.

When they reached her door, she turned around to look at him. Emotions escalated within her. Yearning was becoming a familiar companion. "Would you like to come in?"

"No. If I come in, that practically guarantees that you won't go to bed for at least another half hour, if not longer. I don't want to be responsible if you end up dragging all day tomorrow," he told her, even though the words cost him. "We'll just say good-night right here."

She thought Wyatt meant just that. That he

would leave her right here with only his parting words echoing in his wake.

Rachel didn't want to throw herself at him, but she didn't want the evening to end this way, either.

And while she was thinking about this, debating what move she could make, she suddenly felt his hands framing her face.

The next moment he brought his own down to it.

Her heart began to hammer the moment Wyatt's lips touched hers.

Chapter Fifteen

His kiss was everything she had thought it would be.

And more.

So very much more.

Within moments, Rachel found herself getting lost in the feel of Wyatt's lips against hers, lost in the promise that his mouth was creating within her.

She wrapped her arms around his neck, standing up on her toes and drawing her body up against his almost urgently.

She sighed, enjoying every moment, every nuance that the imprint of his lips created within her.

Before this moment had ever come into fruition, she had thought she would enjoy this—*hoped* that she would enjoy this. But she'd had no idea it would send her spinning out of control the way it did.

Kissing Rachel created a wild excitement within his veins.

Until the sensation had exploded within him, taking him prisoner, Wyatt couldn't have imagined that it would *ever* be like this.

Still framing her face, he found himself drowning in her taste, in her scent, in every single square inch of her.

If he wasn't careful, Wyatt warned himself, he could very easily get carried away.

The kiss grew in intensity, making him want her more than he had *ever* wanted anyone. Wyatt was afraid that if he didn't tear himself away right this instant, he really wouldn't be able to when the time came.

So, exerting incredible control over himself, he drew his lips away and then took a step back.

He saw the quizzical look in her eyes, as if she was silently asking him why he was withdrawing.

"I need to pull away right now," Wyatt told her in a husky whisper.

He felt it was only fair to give her that warning. He wasn't prepared for the look that entered her eyes, which wasn't fear or wariness. Instead, she asked him, "Would that be such a terrible thing?"

He nearly lost it then, nearly gave in to the emotions washing all through him. But then he drew refuge in humor. "It would be if your father decides he wants to make me disappear."

"My father's not like that," she told him with a confident smile.

"Every father is like that when it comes to his daughter," Wyatt said.

She was curious. He sounded like he spoke from experience. "And you know this how?" she asked Wyatt. Had she made a mistake letting herself fall for him? Was he a womanizer after all?

Somehow, she doubted it.

"I read a lot," he deadpanned.

She regarded him for a long moment—and then she laughed. He was putting her on. She should have realized that.

"Of course you do," she said, humoring him. Rachel felt herself wavering. "Are you sure you don't want to come in?"

"No," he answered honestly. "I'm not sure. But I know that I shouldn't. Tell your dad I'll see him tomorrow." Wyatt paused for another moment, lightly brushing his lips against hers.

It was all he trusted himself to do.

"Will do," she replied, watching him retreat toward where he had parked his vehicle.

She stood there for a little while longer, watching him get into his car and then pull out of the development, bound for home.

She was really going to have to watch her step, she told herself.

Rachel remained standing there until there was nothing left for her to watch. A smile flitted across her lips as she squared her shoulders and then walked inside the house.

She had fully expected to find her father asleep in front of the TV the way she had countless other evenings. Instead, she found him not only awake, but apparently eager for details about her evening.

Sitting up ramrod-straight, he asked her, "Did you have a good time?"

The sound of his voice coming out of the blue like that made her jump and swallow a yelp. Rachel placed her hand to her heart, pressing the pounding organ back into place.

"Sorry," George apologized. "I didn't mean to scare you." He looked at her more closely. "Everything all right?"

"Sure. Why shouldn't it be?" she asked him perhaps a little too quickly.

"No reason," he answered. "I just didn't expect to see you home tonight. At least not until it was really late, actually."

Rachel's eyebrows drew together. "Why would you think that?"

A happy smile played on her father's lips. "Well, for one thing, you're a grown woman, and Wyatt is a very handsome young man."

Was her father saying what she thought he was saying? That he had thought she would be sleeping with Wyatt? This was a whole new side to him, Rachel realized.

"Dad!" Rachel cried, surprised and a little taken aback.

"What do you mean?" he questioned his daughter. "It wasn't as if I was born yesterday, or hiding under some rock."

This was way too personal a topic to take up right now and she was in no mood to discuss this with her father. Johanna maybe, but definitely not her father. The man had already had one heart attack. She had no intentions of giving him a second one.

"I'm tired, Dad, and I'm going to bed," Rachel announced.

"Tired?" George repeated, brightening. His smile was almost blinding. "Oh, so then you did—"

He was definitely *not* acting the way she thought he would.

"Good night, Dad. And for your information, I didn't," she informed him tersely before he could finish his question. "See you in the morning."

"All right," he agreed. "Maybe you'll be more inclined to talk to me tomorrow," her father said to her hopefully.

"*Still* won't be anything to talk about then," she informed her father.

George shook his head. "You do know that you're every bit as stubborn as your mother ever was, don't you?" he asked her, not for the first time—or the hundredth. "Maybe even more so."

"So you keep telling me," Rachel remarked, a resigned smile curving her lips.

"So," her father said, putting his hands on the padded sofa arms and then pushing himself up to his feet. "You didn't answer my question," he reminded her. "Did you have a good time?"

There was no reason not to admit to that, as long as he didn't grill her. "Yes, I did," she told him, thinking that would be the end of it.

But she was wrong.

"Were they nice to you?" he asked her.

It didn't take much to figure out who her father was referring to. "Yes, Dad," she told him with a sigh. "They even let me join in all the reindeer games," Rachel said glibly.

"You don't have to get smart, you know," her father chided.

"Yes, I do," she answered, her eyes sparkling. "If I want to keep up with you."

George gave up, shaking his head. "I think that it *is* time for you to be going off to bed," he told her dismissively.

Rachel smiled at him. As far as she was concerned, she had won this round.

"I totally agree," she answered, barely stifling a yawn. She pressed a quick kiss to his cheek. "I'll see you in the morning."

He answered her with the old saying that he used to tell her when she was a little girl. It was like their personal code.

"Not if I see you first."

George's eyes crinkled as he smiled at her. Her less than informative exchange still told him what he wanted to know. That she'd really had a good time.

He felt heartened.

He had made the right choice, turning the matter of finding someone for his daughter over to Maizie in the first place.

With any luck, he mused, he would be dancing at his daughter's wedding before the year was out.

After he'd had his heart attack, his principal concern was that Rachel would be taken care of if something did happen to him.

Only then would he be able to relax. Because at that point, if she did have a husband, or at least someone she cared about in her life, it didn't really matter what became of him.

That fine young man would watch out for her, he thought as he made his way up the stairs,

George was smiling as he got into bed.

Rachel had been certain that she would immediately drop off to sleep the moment she crawled into bed and pulled the covers up.

But she had thought wrong.

It seemed as if her body and her mind were conspiring against her, inexplicably rousing her every time she was about to drift off to sleep. It was then that her mind would completely fill up with thoughts that insisted on setting her body on fire.

After twenty minutes of unsuccessful attempts to fall asleep, Rachel sat up and dragged her hand through her hair.

This was ridiculous.

Thoughts of Wyatt played through her head, taunting her with visions of what might have been if he hadn't stepped back and she *had* taken him up on the silent promise his body had made.

No, she chided herself. She couldn't just hop into bed with the first good-looking man who smiled at her and made her body sizzle because he had kissed her. There had to be more to it than that.

How would you know if there's more if you don't give it a chance? Rachel asked herself.

She had no answer for that.

Tossing and turning as she searched for a comfortable spot, Rachel finally fell asleep several hours later.

Just before dawn.

When the morning came, she woke up to find that she was even more exhausted than when she had first fallen asleep.

But there was no time for her to stay in bed and try to grab a few more winks of sleep. She had to get up. Rachel wanted to make a hasty escape before her father declared that breakfast was waiting and definitely before Wyatt showed up to give her father his physical therapy session.

Despite her good intentions, she wound up bumping into Wyatt just as she was about to make a hasty exit.

"Wow," Wyatt said, taking a long look at her face. She looked really tired, he thought, instantly feeling guilty. He should have brought her home earlier. "Did you get any sleep last night?"

"Some," she answered with a careless shrug. It was a lie and they both knew it.

"You do know that if you lie, your nose is going to grow, right?" Wyatt asked her, watching her face intently as he walked into the foyer.

"My nose is my own affair," she told him dismissively. And then she realized how that had to have sounded to him. She wasn't usually that curt. "Sorry, my father already gave me the third degree when I walked in last night. I'm afraid that he set the tone for the rest of the night—and, it looks like, the following day, as well."

He wondered what she had told her father about their late night. "Should we be getting our stories straight?" he asked her.

Rachel shook her head. "No, no stories. Just the truth," she told him. She had always found that it was much simpler that way. Sticking to the truth whenever it was possible.

"Wow," he said in admiration, "you really are one admirable lady."

"I just don't believe in lying if I can avoid it," she told him. "Keeping a story straight is far easier when it's the truth."

His smile widened. "Like I said, one really admirable lady," he told her. And then he turned on his heel, watching her as she began to leave the house. “Hey, listen,” Wyatt called after her.

She turned to look at him. She really didn't want to interact with her father this morning. Not until her face stopped looking like thirty miles of bad road.

“Yes?”

“Would you be up for a date this weekend?” Wyatt asked, catching her totally by surprise. She turned back and took a few steps toward him. “One of my friends is having a barbecue and I thought that since we've broken the ‘dating ice,’ so to speak, maybe you'd like to go with me. They're really nice people. And it won't be nearly as crowded as my sister's anniversary celebration was.”

When she didn't answer right away he wondered if she thought he was attempting to pressure her, or moving too fast.

“It's not mandatory, but I'd really like you to come,” he told her. His eyes met hers, coaxing her. “How about it?”

“I'd love to,” she finally replied. “And it'll give you and my father something to talk about during your exercise session with him.”

Wyatt didn't quite follow her reasoning. “Come again?”

“I get the distinct impression that my father is worried that I'm about to become an old maid—his idea of an old maid," she clarified. She had no idea what the modern version of that was these days. Did people even think in those terms anymore?

Wyatt shook his head. "You're not anyone's idea of an old maid."

That made her smile for a second.

And then, the next moment Rachel heard her father coming down the stairs. He'd gotten a late start, she thought.

"Looks like it's time for me to beat a hasty retreat," she told him "before I have to submit to another version of the Spanish Inquisition."

"That bad?" Wyatt asked her.

"That bad," she responded. *Well, maybe not quite*, she mentally amended, but she hated having to answer questions and account for herself. She always had. "Good luck today."

"Why would I need luck?" he asked, his eyes following her.

"Do you think I'm the only one he's going to subject to a huge question-and-answer period?" she asked Wyatt. The expression on her face negated any doubts he might have about that.

"Rachel?" she heard her father call out. "Are you down here?"

She looked undecided as she glanced over her shoulder. "So much for my hasty retreat," she lamented.

"Your father's not about to quiz you in front of me," he told her.

"I didn't think of you as being naive. My father would quiz me in front of *everyone*, and anyone," she told Wyatt. She started to go, but he suddenly caught her arm. When she looked at him with an unspoken question in her eyes, he said, "I'm looking forward to going to the barbecue with you."

I'm looking forward to just being with you, she thought. But out loud she gave him a nonchalant "Yes, that'll be fun."

His eyes met hers. "I'll give you the details later this week."

"And the drama continues," she murmured under her breath.

"Rachel," he called after her a second time.

This time, feeling slightly impatient because she wanted to leave before her father came down, she turned to look at him. "Yes?"

In response, Wyatt kissed her, quickly and with feeling, then told her, "Go, before your father gets down here."

Rachel didn't have to be told twice.

Smiling broadly, she was gone by the time her father entered the hallway.

Chapter Sixteen

As she sailed in through Vesuvius's front door, Rachel braced herself for an interrogation from Johanna.

But there was none.

To Rachel's surprise and relief, Johanna had broken an age-old tradition. She hadn't come in early.

Or at all.

With any luck, Rachel could sequester herself in the supply closet and do whatever needed to be done without having to put up with a barrage of questions about what happened at the anniversary celebration yesterday.

However, before very long, the quiet began to get to her.

Quickly.

Rachel kept looking at her watch. And that kept interfering with her getting anything done.

After an hour had dragged by, she went out into the main dining area, which, at this hour, was exceedingly quiet.

"Has anyone heard from Johanna?" she asked the staff members who were busy setting up for the first shift.

The five people there met her question with bewildered shakes of their heads.

"We thought she would have called you," Janice, one of the older servers, told Rachel. "She didn't?"

Just to be certain—maybe her phone had somehow reverted to silent mode—Rachel took out her cell phone and checked. But there had been no missed call.

Rachel shook her head. "Nope, she didn't call." Now she was really concerned.

She quickly began to input the woman's number. The only answer she got was Johanna's voice mail, which cheerfully told her to "please leave a message."

This was not like Johanna, Rachel thought, growing more and more worried. At a loss as to what to do, she was about to try again when she heard her father's voice as he walked in. It was obvious that he was talking to someone.

She hurried toward the sound of her father's voice.

"Dad," she began before she had a chance to even reach him, "have you heard from—Johanna?" Her voice trailed off as she realized that her father had actually come in with Johanna and was speaking to her right at this moment.

"As a matter of fact," he told his daughter with a smile that was directed at the woman who was with him, "I have."

Since Johanna had made it a practice of always being early and had never come in late or even missed a day in all the years she had been working at Vesuvius, Rachel was torn between relief and annoyance at having been put through this in the first place. She settled for asking the woman, "Is everything all right, Johanna?" quickly followed by "Where have you been?" which came out a little more sharply than she had intended.

"Well, for the first half hour, I was sitting in my car, trying to start a dead battery," the assistant manager told Rachel. She slanted a smile toward George. Rachel could see that the man was nothing short of her hero. "And then your father picked me up."

Rachel realized that her father was beaming.

"It's been a long time since I've ridden to the rescue," he told his daughter with pride.

She glanced at her watch again to confirm what she was about to ask. "Aren't you supposed to be home, doing your exercises with Wyatt right now?"

"When Johanna called, Wyatt gave me a pass," he informed her. "He thinks that since I've made so much progress lately, it was all right if I cut one session short. He told me it was okay with him, seeing as how I had a really good reason."

More points for the golden boy, Rachel thought, knowing that Wyatt had managed to raise his stock even more in her father's eyes with this latest move.

Rachel looked more closely at Johanna. "Are you sure that you're all right?"

"Other than wanting to take a sledgehammer to my car, I'm fine," the older woman replied.

"Why didn't you call me?" Rachel asked. "I would have been more than happy to come to get you, Johanna."

But Johanna waved her hand at the mere suggestion. "You have more than enough to handle. Besides, it all turned out all right. Your dad had my car towed to his mechanic." She took a deep breath, trying to put the whole experience behind her for now. "Well, I'd better get to work. Too much time has gone by."

With that, she turned toward the locker room and began heading in that general direction.

Rachel turned toward her father, who for once had been silently listening to this exchange.

"I guess maybe I should stop worrying about you," she told him.

"Oh, honey," George chided her, "a daughter should never have to worry about her father. It's the other way around." Worry, in his opinion, was strictly a one-way road.

"Where is that written?" Rachel challenged.

He shrugged carelessly, a smile playing on his lips. "I dunno. But I'm sure that it is written somewhere," he told her. "You know, it felt really good being useful again."

She realized what he meant and shook her head. "Dad, you're always useful."

"Yeah, yeah," he said, waving his hand at her comment. "I mean really."

"So do I," she told him. And then her tone softened. "I'll make you a deal, Dad. You stop worrying about me and I'll stop worrying about you. How's that?"

George laughed. "Sounds good to me," he said. "Well, my kitchen awaits." Turning to look at Rachel, he asked, "It is still my kitchen, right?"

"It always has been, Dad," Rachel told him. Her words coaxed a smile from her father.

She watched as he disappeared into the kitchen, then went toward the locker room to make sure that Johanna was none the worse for her experience. She knew the woman wasn't one to complain, especially to her father.

Rachel all but walked into the assistant manager as she was in the process of coming out.

Seeing her, the first words out of Johanna's mouth were "So, how was last night? Did he light up your life?" A smile curved her lips as she asked the questions.

Rachel sighed, shaking her head. "And to think I was worried about you."

"Don't try to play innocent," Johanna told her. "I want to hear details, lots of details."

The latter fixed the older woman with a look. "There's nothing to tell, Johanna."

"Don't give me that, I've known you ever since you were a little bitty thing. And let's not forget, I have eyes, Rachel. I've seen the way you two look at each other. There was nothing indifferent about the looks you two exchanged. So be honest with me. How was it?"

Rachel blew out a breath. She couldn't seem to get Johanna to back off, but then, she really hadn't expected to.

"I had a nice time," Rachel said. "From all indications, so did he."

That was obviously not enough to satisfy Johanna. "And?"

"And when it was over," Rachel continued stubbornly, "Wyatt took me home."

"*His* home?" Johanna asked, her face lighting up.

"No, *my* home," Rachel emphasized. "You and I both know that if I was late coming home, my father would have called out the National Guard and had them all out looking for me." Her father did not do things in a half-hearted manner.

"I'm not too sure about that," Johanna told her as she began to walk away.

Rachel quickly caught up to the older woman. "You know something I don't?" she asked, trying to get a handle on all of this.

Johanna eyed her innocently. "I'm just an observer of human nature, dear," the older woman replied. "Now if you'll excuse me, since you're not coming forth with details—"

"There *aren't* any details to come 'forth' with," Rachel insisted, shooting a meaningful look in Johanna's direction.

"As I said, I have work to catch up on." The woman paused one last time and asked, "Did he at least ask you out again?"

In self-defense, Rachel almost said, "No." But she had never believed in lying, and she had a feeling that Johanna would somehow find out anyway. She really didn't want to be caught in a lie.

"Yes," Rachel answered, gritting her teeth together, knowing that this laid the groundwork for round two. "Satisfied?"

The assistant manager surprised her by saying "No, but I'm getting there." A smile filtered into her eyes. "We'll talk later."

"Oh, goody, something to look forward to," Rachel quipped sarcastically.

And then she added, "I'm really glad you're all right, Johanna."

"Don't worry about me. I'm invincible," Johanna said, proceeding to wave the younger woman away. "Now, shoo. I've got work to do."

The rest of the week went by in more or less of a blur. Because she had gone out with Wyatt on Saturday, Rachel felt as if she had a great deal to catch up on both at work and in her studies.

She did her best, but even so, she found that something had to be sacrificed. It was either catching up, or sleeping. She wasn't able to do both—but she did really try hard.

She would have felt a lot better mentally if she had managed to catch up with her work and her classes, but despite the fact that it would have made her feel a great deal better about the situation, it just wasn't something that she was able to do.

She still interacted with Wyatt. It occurred to her that he came to the house early—early enough for them to at least say a few words to each other before she went on to work at the restaurant and Wyatt began to work with her father.

After the sessions were over, of course, Wyatt would drop off her father at the restaurant. This way, her father wouldn't feel as if he was exerting himself, and just as important, Wyatt and Rachel could see one another before they went on to work for the rest of their day.

And then, before she knew it, it was Saturday again. As much as she was looking forward to spending more time with Wyatt than just small snatches here and there, Rachel didn't feel as if she really had the luxury of being able to do that.

Every moment of her day felt as if it was jam-packed with things to do.

On her way to do something, Johanna stopped and doubled back to look at Rachel. "Why do you look as if you're about to start sucking on a lemon?" she asked, taking Rachel's expression into account. "Correct me if I'm wrong, but aren't you going out this afternoon with Wyatt?"

"Well, I was supposed to," Rachel told Johanna, measuring out her words slowly.

"But…?" the woman said, attempting to coax an explanation out of her.

"But now I'm thinking that maybe I should use the time to try to catch up on my studies. I've really fallen behind," Rachel told her.

Out of the corner of her eye, she saw her father approaching them. Suddenly, she felt herself being ambushed.

"Honey, the studies will always be there," George told his daughter.

"Dad, I've got to catch up sometime," Rachel argued. And the longer she took, the further behind she would fall.

Rather than continue arguing, her father tried another tactic, "Did I ever tell you that your mother took off six months before she went on to complete her nursing degree?"

This was news to Rachel and she wondered if her father was making the whole thing up.

"She did? She never said anything to me about that. Why would she have taken the time off?" Rachel asked. She noticed that Johanna had grown quiet, letting her father do all the talking.

A nostalgic smile flitted across her father's lips. "Well, for the first two months," he remembered, "it was because she was at the end of her pregnancy with you. The last four months after that, she felt it was more important for her to be your mother than for her to be there for other people, attending to them.

"There's no arguing that your mother was a damn fine nurse, but she always knew her priorities." He looked at Rachel over the large pan of baked ziti he had just prepared. "Am I making myself clear?" Then, when Rachel didn't respond, he told her, "Sometimes knowing how to focus on what's more important and ignoring what are just details that might get in the way will help make you a better nurse."

Rachel had trouble hiding her amusement. She could see what her father was trying to do. "Are you saying that going out with Wyatt is going to help me be a better nurse?"

"I'm saying that all work and no play make Rachel not only a dull girl, but an exhausted one," her father emphasized. "Prioritize, Rachel. Prioritize."

She understood what he was trying to do and she appreciated his concern, but he didn't understand what it was going to cost her.

"If I keep going at this rate, Dad, I'm never going to graduate."

"Oh, sure you are," George said, waving away her concern. "I have great faith in you. You always finish what you start—just like your mother did." His eyes crinkled as he smiled at his daughter. "She would have liked Wyatt. Now go home, kid, and get ready."

"It's not like I have to dress up," she protested. "It's a barbecue."

"All right, go home and get dressed down," her father told her, humor curving his mouth. "Just make yourself scarce and go."

She laughed, surrendering. It wasn't much of a battle anyway since she really did want to attend this with Wyatt. Part of her had been looking forward to it all week.

But she couldn't just let her father win without some sort of a comment. "If I didn't know any better, I'd say you were trying to get rid of me."

His eyes met hers. "Good guess," her father told her. "Now go," he urged. "And bring me home a spare rib."

"How do you know what they're serving?"

He smiled at her over his shoulder. "Wyatt told me, of course."

"Oh?" She looked at her father curiously. "What else did Wyatt tell you?"

He looked at her, innocence personified. "Men don't betray a trust," he told his daughter. "You should know that."

She laughed, shaking her head. There was no two ways about it. Wyatt was definitely good for her father. Not only had he gotten her father capable of moving around far more easily these days, but he had done wonders for her father's mind, as well. Always preoccupied and working at a fever pitch, her father was responding far better now than before he had had his attack. And she was grateful that his sense of humor was back.

And it seemed to mean a lot to her father that she went on to see Wyatt outside the parameters of their day-to-day relationship.

Not that that was any sort of hardship for her.

The overprotective daughter belatedly rose to the surface, although she was getting better at keeping that side of herself under wraps these days. Looking around the kitchen, she asked her father, "Are you sure you can handle everything?"

For a moment, he looked as if he was going to say something else, but then his eyes crinkled with humor as he said, "Somehow, I think I'll manage. *Now* will you finally go?"

"Okay, okay, I'm going," she told him, then reminded her father, "Just remember, this was your idea, Dad."

The grin nearly split his face. "I won't forget."

There was something in her father's voice that she couldn't quite put her finger on, but it sounded a little bit like mischievous glee.

The next moment, grabbing her purse, Rachel quickly made her way out of the restaurant.

She had a barbecue to get to.

Chapter Seventeen

Leaving her car parked on one side of the three-car driveway, Rachel locked it and ran into the house, heart hammering fast.

She had to stop cutting it so close, she silently lectured herself. One unforeseen traffic jam and all of her plans would have been totally thrown off.

But Rachel had put her fate in the hands of the traffic gods and prayed that if any car was going to break down or had the misfortune of running into another vehicle, it wouldn't happen until she had cleared that area.

Other than hearing an awful, bone-chilling noise

that suddenly came from beneath her car's hood when she took a turn far too quickly and sharply, nothing else went wrong. She made it home without any awful mishaps. Not only that, but it was still just under the time she had allotted herself.

If she had working brain cells, Rachel told herself, she would have laid out the clothes earlier, maybe last night, or at least before she had left for work this morning. But running on what amounted to a super-tight schedule—was there any other kind?—kept her from thinking too far ahead. And that, at least for the time being, kept her from getting nervous.

Telling herself that everything was going to go well now didn't really help matters. Going to the barbecue was different from the celebration she had attended with Wyatt last week. As near as she could tell, there wasn't going to be any dancing or crowds of people to disappear into until she could get her bearings, like there had been last time.

This was more a situation where she was going to have to hit the ground running and just hope for the best.

She was up for that, right, Rachel silently asked herself as she locked the door behind her.

She knew enough not to answer that honestly.

Taking a deep breath, Rachel bounded up the stairs, flew to her room and threw open the closet. She wasn't even sure what she was going to find there. With everything that had gone on in the last two years, it had been a while since she had actually rummaged through her closet.

Moving articles of clothing around, she honed in on a pair of form-fitting navy blue shorts and a red-and-white checkered, short-sleeved, short-waisted shirt. The outfit wasn't exactly spectacular, Rachel thought, but somehow it did seem appropriate to her for a barbecue.

She changed into the shorts and shirt quickly.

What actually occupied her mind first and foremost, more than finding something to wear, was being able to bring something with her to the barbecue. Maybe it was the business she had grown up in, but it absolutely didn't seem right to her to show up in response to an invitation empty-handed.

Looking around in the refrigerator, Rachel immediately saw the foil-covered pan of baked ziti. She peeked under the foil and saw that the pan was entirely untouched. Her father had to have been experimenting with different cheeses and additives last night. He had a habit of never wanting his recipe to turn out exactly the same way twice in a row.

Very carefully, Rachel slipped the pan into the oven and set to warm for fifteen minutes.

While it was warming up, she went to the cupboard and took out the red padded case she used on occasion to transport meals, either to or from the restaurant. It was a safe way to carry the pan and it kept the heat in.

She had just finished depositing the warmed-up ziti into the carrying case when she heard the doorbell ring.

After stripping off her gloves, she glanced at her watch and sighed. The man was uncanny. He was right on the dot. She had a feeling that it was a habit ingrained in him from a young age by his mother. Ariel Watson didn't remind her of a woman who tolerated lateness.

Pulling off the apron she had hastily donned, Rachel made her way over to the front door, opened it and smiled up at Wyatt.

"Hi, you're right on time as always," Rachel told him.

Wyatt took a good look at her. The woman had legs that just didn't seem to quit, he thought, looking at the way the shorts fit her. He hadn't realized just how gorgeous she could look in shorts.

"And you," he responded belatedly, his eyes devouring her, "look really delicious." The words replayed themselves in his ears and he flushed slightly. "Sorry," he apologized, "that came out before I could censor myself."

Rachel could feel heat rising to her cheeks. It

wasn't that she didn't like being complimented, she just didn't know how to respond.

Looking at the floor, she shrugged. "I guess I can forgive you," she murmured.

"Oh, good, that takes a weight off my mind," he quipped, in turn flashing a wicked grin at her.

Feeling he should come in just in case she wasn't ready to leave yet, Wyatt took two steps into the house. He was immediately struck by the aroma that was wafting all around, teasing his taste buds and making him all but salivate.

"What is that fantastic smell?" he asked. He took in another deep breath, trying to zero in on the aroma and pinpoint what it was. He knew her father was working at the restaurant. That left just her. He looked at Rachel in surprise. "Have you been cooking?" Wyatt asked. Why would she do that? They were going to be eating at his friends' house. "I told you I was taking you to a barbecue."

"Yes, I know," she answered. "And I thought it was only right to bring something with me."

"You are," Wyatt told her with a smile. Spreading his arms out, he inclined his head and told her, "You're bringing me."

"I know," she answered. "But this will be a bit tastier."

She indicated the food carrier into which she'd packed the pan of baked ziti. She knew her father wouldn't mind her taking it. He was the one who had taught her not to show up empty-handed if she was invited anywhere.

Wyatt's eyes held hers for a long moment and his mouth curved. "Are you sure about that?" he asked in a voice she couldn't call anything but sexy.

Rachel could feel herself responding to the tall well-built man, but this was neither the time nor the place to give in. She had a feeling that if she did, even just for a moment, they would never make it to the barbecue.

Or even out the door.

"I think we need to go," she told Wyatt, taking a step back to put at least a little distance between them. "My father maintains that if you're invited somewhere, it's rude to turn up late."

Her back to Wyatt now, she made sure that the zipper was secure all the way around the carrier. It would be terrible—not to mention an awful waste—to have the contents of the pan come tumbling out, sending everything straight to the ground.

"I'll carry that out for you," Wyatt volunteered, "but when we get to the barbecue, you're going to have to help me beat back my friends."

She looked at him quizzically. "One whiff of this and I guarantee they'll forget all about the barbecue."

""That doesn't sound as if you think all that

much of this barbecue," she told him. "Or the barbecuing abilities of the person in charge of it." She had to have misunderstood him.

"Well, to be honest, I don't. I mean, we're not going to be poisoned or anything," he said quickly. "But we get together for the camaraderie of the thing, not the food." He nodded down at the carrier in his hands, saying, "At least until now." He grinned at her as they walked to his vehicle. "If I know my friends, once they sample that baked ziti, they're going to insist I bring you to all our gatherings from now on."

He was getting carried away, she thought. "Why don't we see how they feel about it first?" Rachel suggested. "They might hate it—or feel as if I was trying to show up the host—or hostess."

The moment the words were out of her mouth, she suddenly realized the import of what she was saying. "They won't think that, will they?" she asked, worried, as she got in on her side.

Wyatt placed the red carrier with the baked ziti pan on the back seat behind the driver's side. He pulled a seat belt around it, all but tucking it in to make sure the carrier wouldn't go flying toward the front if he came to an unexpected, sudden stop.

Finished, he shook his head as he came around

to the driver's seat. "You realize that you worry way too much, don't you?"

It wasn't a criticism, it was meant to help calm her down.

"No, I don't," she protested. Then, in a quieter voice, she murmured with a shrug, "I don't get out on my own that much."

"You won't be out on your own," he quickly reminded her. "I'll be with you—and it will all be fine. You look great," he emphasized again. "And the aroma from the baked ziti will anesthetize all of them. Hard for anyone to be the least bit unfriendly when they're salivating," he told her.

Rachel laughed. She didn't know how Wyatt managed to do it, but the man did have a way of saying things that just made her feel good inside. Not to mention that he made her laugh.

And it really did make her feel good to laugh.

Rachel settled back in her seat, finally getting comfortable.

"So tell me about these people at the barbecue," she asked. She wanted to be prepared just in case there might be surprises. She didn't want to get blindsided if it turned out that one of the women there had been engaged to Wyatt at one time, or that they had a history that went way back.

He thought for a moment, sifting through information. Glancing at Rachel, he shook his head. "Not much to tell. There'll be six of them there this afternoon. Adam, Jenny, Mike, Lucy, Gordon and Cindy," he enumerated.

"And you?" she questioned. Did he realize that the way he put it made him the odd man in this gathering? Four guys and three women. Had it always been that way, or was there a fourth woman who was no longer included in their ranks?

"And me," he answered with a nod. "We all went to elementary school together, so we go way back."

"The way you went over their names, you made it sound as if they were paired off," she pointed out, wondering if that was on purpose, or if it was just the way he thought of them.

"They are," he told her. "Now. It didn't start out that way, though. But looking back, I guess it was kind of inevitable. I think that they were perfect for one another," he said, remembering certain instances.

That led her to feel that his friends could only come to one conclusion when they walked in. "Does that mean that they are going to think that we're a couple?"

"We're just friends," he said quickly, not because he thought that, but because he felt she would be more comfortable if it was presented that way.

But after a moment, he knew he had to ask. "Would it bother you if they thought we were?"

"I'd want to know how you felt about it first," she told him without hesitation.

She was hedging, he thought, and he didn't know if that was for self-preservation, or because she was trying to get him to commit himself first.

Two could play that game. "Depends on how you felt," he countered.

She couldn't help but laugh. "We're going to dance around this all afternoon, aren't we?"

"Maybe. Maybe not," he said with a wide smile as he slanted a glance in her direction. "Do you have a preference which it is?"

She did. But she didn't want to scare him off or say anything that might jeopardize the possible relationship what was, if anything, still in its infancy.

"I do," she whispered.

The words skimmed along his neck, warming him. Tantalizing him. He found himself wishing that they were going to his place instead of to his friends' barbecue. "But you're not going to tell me?" he guessed.

"Not yet." Her smile was wide and seemed to tell him things her words couldn't. "Let's see how the baked ziti goes over."

"Well, if that's the criterion, you might as well

get used to the commitment, because I can tell you right now, none of my friends were born without taste buds. One deep breath—forget about actually taking a bite out of what you just brought over—and I guarantee that they'll be yours for life."

"Let's just wait and see," she told him.

"Whatever makes you happy," he said cheerfully. "But I can tell you now, they'll love the ziti."

She nodded, thinking that Wyatt was being a little too optimistic. "Is there anything else I should know?"

"Other than letting yourself have a good time?" he asked pointedly.

"Yes, other than that."

He shook his head. "I can't think of a thing offhand—or on hand," he added, aiming a look in her direction.

She pressed her lips together to keep the rest of her questions under wraps for now. She didn't want him to grow annoyed—not that he ever had, but there was always a first time.

They arrived at their destination within ten minutes.

She saw that there were several cars in the driveway. That made it necessary to park a little ways down by the curb. The moment he stopped his car and they got out, they heard loud voices—and deep laughter.

It sounded as if everyone there was having a good time.

"Looks like everyone's here," Wyatt told her, pausing to uncouple the seat belt in the back seat so he could take the carrier with Rachel's contribution to the festivities out of the vehicle.

Rachel paused to listen. "That sounds like a lot more people than just six," she told him.

Wyatt laughed. "They have a tendency to sound like they're a crowd," he agreed, "but trust me, what you're hearing is just six very loud, very happy people enjoying each other's company."

With the carrier secure in both hands, Wyatt nodded toward Rachel. "Ready?" he asked.

"Why wouldn't I be?" she asked even as she took in a deep breath.

Wyatt bent his head in closer toward her. "It might help if you didn't look as if you were braced to swallow a dose of some awful, gut-wrenching medicine. Trust me, my friends are all harmless. Every single one of them," he promised, adding, "You're going to have fun. Besides, they'll all be too busy eating the baked ziti you brought to even notice that you're wearing two different shoes."

Her eyes widened and her mouth dropped open. "I am?" she cried before she had a chance to even look down at her feet.

She wasn't.

He had the good grace not to laugh, at least not out loud, when she shot him a dirty look.

"No, you're not. Rachel, you really have to learn how to relax. I've got an idea. We're going to make going out a weekly thing until you get comfortable enough not to think of it as a big deal." And then he added, "You've just become my new project."

She sincerely doubted that she would *ever* get comfortable enough going out with him *not* to think of it as a big deal.

Out loud she informed him, "I'm not a project."

"Oh, I kind of think you are," Wyatt countered, his eyes shining as they swept over her very slowly. "A really nice, interesting project."

What was *that* supposed to mean? The question hammered in her mind. She was about to ask for an explanation.

And then the front door suddenly opened. The voices grew louder. There was no more time for an argument—or a discussion, depending on how either of them viewed the verbal exchange.

Chapter Eighteen

"Hi, stranger, nice to know that you're still among the living," the petite brunette who had answered the door declared.

Grinning, Jenny Russell attempted to give Wyatt, whom she had known ever since she was a very little girl, a quick, enthusiastic hug. But she discovered that he had something large and cumbersome in his hands that blocked her quick display of affection.

Taking a step back, the young woman looked at what had stopped her full-on embrace.

"And you've come bearing gifts—or food, by the smell of it," she concluded with a delighted laugh.

"Actually, this is Rachel's donation to the festivities. She made this," Wyatt told his friend, nodding at the carrier. And then he quickly made the necessary introductions before either woman could ask. "Jenny, this is Rachel Fenelli. Rachel, this is my really good friend Jenny Russell."

Not standing on ceremony, Jenny was already giving Rachel a warm hug. Wyatt's friend's face completely lit up as she smiled.

"Welcome to my home. You are staying for the barbecue, aren't you?" Jenny asked as she wove her arm through Rachel's.

Without missing a beat, Jenny then guided her new guest into the house and, subsequently, toward the rather spacious backyard.

"That's the general idea," Wyatt answered. "That's why she brought along her offering to the barbecue."

"That smells heavenly," Jenny proclaimed, taking in a long, deep breath. "What is it and where did you get it?" she asked with genuine interest.

"It's baked ziti," Rachel told her. "And it's from my father's restaurant. He's the one who made it."

Jenny stopped walking just as she moved back the sliding glass door that led into the backyard. "You're kidding. Your father *made* this? Really?" she cried, visibly impressed.

"Rachel has never been known to lie," Wyatt told his friend.

The way Wyatt had structured his statement, he made it sound as if they had known one another for a very long time instead of for such a short duration. She had to admit that she rather liked that. Liked the idea it conveyed. Not because she was trying to impress his friends, but because she liked the thought that he was the one who felt that way.

Rather than say anything to Wyatt in response, Jenny called out to the other people who were gathered in her yard.

"Hey, everybody, look who I found on my front step!" The five people immediately began calling out greetings to Wyatt as they gathered around him—as well as the woman they didn't know yet. "This is Rachel," Jenny informed her friends. "And she brought food to appease us until Adam can finally get the barbecue started."

She flashed a smile at the tall blond man she was referring to.

"Yeah, provided he's finally gotten the hang of lighting those 'tricky' little barbecue coals," another man laughed.

When Rachel turned to look at who was talking, her mouth promptly fell open. The man who had just made the comment looked like the exact double of the man Jenny had called "Adam."

She heard Wyatt laugh behind her. When she looked at him quizzically, he slipped his arm around her waist and apologized as he gave her a quick hug.

"Sorry, you just looked really surprised," Wyatt told her, then went on to explain, "You see, Adam and Mike are identical twins."

She didn't like being caught off guard like that. "I'm sorry. I thought my eyes were playing tricks on me," she told Wyatt.

"Don't worry about it," Jenny told her with a dismissive wave of her hand. "Just think about how I feel."

"And me," another pretty woman, a vibrant redhead with clear-water blue eyes spoke up as she stepped forward. "I'm married to this one," she told Rachel as she hooked her arm through Mike's. "And in the beginning, he liked to mess with my mind and tell me he was his brother." She smiled at Rachel. "Hi, I'm Lucy, Mike's better half," she declared with feeling as she introduced herself to Rachel.

"And we're Cindy and Gordon," a third woman, this one with chestnut brown, shoulder-length hair and a spectacular figure, said as she and the man whose hand she was holding moved a step closer toward Rachel. "We're originals," Cindy told her with an amused laugh. "And you are…?" Cindy left her sentence open-ended as she looked at Rachel, waiting. It was obvious that she hadn't caught the young woman's name.

"Clearly overwhelmed," Rachel answered, looking around.

She hadn't meant to make the others laugh, but that wound up being the upshot of her reply and she discovered that the honest summation turned out to be a really good icebreaker.

That, coupled with the baked ziti she had brought to the barbecue, endeared her to the others and cemented her place in the group.

Wyatt looked on, pleased. It was obvious that he felt this was all going well.

Several questions and exchanges later, Rachel glanced over in his direction and saw that Wyatt was still quietly watching her. Seeing her, he leaned forward so that only she could hear him and said, "Looks like you can relax now."

However, Jenny overheard him. About to go get refills for a round of wine coolers, she stopped for a moment to comment, "Of course she can relax now. Why shouldn't she be able to relax?" Jenny challenged.

Turning toward Rachel, their hostess said,

"You know, you're the first one that Wyatt has ever brought to one of our gatherings. Half the time he'd beg off, saying he was too busy working to come. But the other half of the time he would come solo. My theory, if you ask me—"

"No one asked, Jenny," Wyatt told her.

His friend continued as if she hadn't been interrupted. "I think that's a reaction to his sister, mother and at one point, his sister-in-law all trying to fix him up with their friends." She directed a sympathetic look Wyatt's way. "The poor guy got really worn out and just wanted to spend some quality time with his buddies," she said, gesturing around to include the entire gathering. And then, smiling at Rachel, she said, "Welcome to the buddy circle, Rachel."

Rachel felt as if she had passed some sort of initiation ritual without even knowing it. And she had a feeling that this had just made Wyatt uncomfortable. She wasn't about to sit back and let that feeling fester, so she did her best to shift the focus of attention away from Wyatt.

"What can I do to help?" she asked, looking at Jenny.

"Come with me," Jenny said, looking happy at the offer.

"Took you long enough," the woman mouthed

to Wyatt just before she walked off to the kitchen with Rachel. "But you really got a good one."

Rachel had assumed from the way Wyatt had first painted the barbecue that the event would last a couple of hours, and then, winding down, it would be over.

But if anything, the conversation only progressed and blossomed, hopping from one topic to another as naturally as a frog making its way from one lily pad to another as he made his way across a pond.

Rachel was fascinated as well as entertained.

At times she found that Wyatt's friends—as well as Wyatt himself—ended each other's sentences. Remarkable though she found it, it seemed that they were that tuned in to one another, to what each person in the group might be thinking.

She couldn't help envying them.

It had to be really nice having friends like this. His friends were practically like family, she caught herself wistfully thinking.

It certainly didn't take much to detect the warmth that was there, both on the surface as well as just beneath it.

She wondered if Wyatt knew how lucky he was or how rare the situation was.

* * *

"They like you," Wyatt told her at one point as twilight began to wrap itself around the gathering.

He brought over a tall, frosty glass of diet soda she had requested and set it down in front of her. Initially she had asked if there was any, because she was going to go fetch her own, but he had told her to stay put, that he would go get it for her.

Rachel liked the way Wyatt responded to her. Liked his willingness to get up and fetch what she needed. Her mother had been like that with her father on occasion, and her father had reciprocated in kind, as well. To her that was a sign of a good relationship.

But she herself had never been on the receiving end of that sort of behavior.

It felt nice, she couldn't help thinking.

"And I like them," Rachel answered, taking a sip of her drink.

She wasn't just mouthing what she felt Wyatt wanted to hear. She meant what she said. Not only that, but the way his friends seemed to accept her really heartened her. At first, she thought it might all be pretense in order not to make any waves because they all seemed to care about Wyatt.

But she found that they—mainly the women—were nice to her when Wyatt was elsewhere and had no way of knowing if they were treating her well or not. He was busy talking to the guys on some topic or other.

As this continued through the evening, Rachel almost felt as if she was dreaming.

And now Wyatt was telling her what she had suspected and hoped for the last few hours—that his friends liked her. It wasn't the syrupy, air-kissing kind of "like" built on a foundation of falsity, which meant really less than nothing.

This, she thought, came across like a genuine regard, built on questions and answers that had been exchanged and accumulated over the course of the day. Maybe it wasn't rock-solid yet, but it was definitely getting there, she felt.

"I knew you'd all hit it off," Wyatt told her as they all sat comfortably out on the patio in the cooling evening breeze. "Otherwise, I wouldn't have brought you together. Besides, if they didn't like you, this wouldn't have worked out."

"You mean you would have dropped me if they voted me out of their club?" she asked, not entirely sure just what he was telling her.

"No, it wasn't anything like that," he said, looking surprised that she would actually think that. "But we all have similar tastes, similar responses to people. If they hadn't taken to you, it would have just made me take a closer look at us."

"Us," she repeated, rolling the word around on her tongue. "Is there an 'us'?" Rachel finally asked him.

Was she questioning their relationship, or just fishing for something? "You don't think so?"

Oh no. She wasn't about to coach him. She wanted Wyatt to give her a straight answer. "I asked you first."

He had a feeling that he could see right through her. "You know, no one's going to hold it against you if you drop your guard just this once," he told her.

"If I drop my guard, I could get run over," she told him honestly.

She could have sworn she saw a flash of affection in his eyes. "I promise not to let anyone run you over."

"What if you're the one who's doing the running over?" Rachel asked, cocking her head as she studied Wyatt.

He smiled at her. "That's simple enough to answer. I won't be," he told her. "Ever." His eyes met hers and he closed his arms around her shoulders in a protective gesture. "I promise."

"You know I can't hold you to that," she told

him. He could change on her at any time if he wanted to. Elliott had taught her that. He hadn't been perfect, heaven knows, but she'd believed he was basically honest—until he wasn't.

"Sure you can. I'm an honorable guy. Just ask any of my friends here," he told her, nodding toward the circle of people sitting around them. All of them, at the moment, looked as if they were on the verge of contently dropping off to sleep.

"I don't think that they would make such good material witnesses right now," Rachel told him. "They look like they're about to fall asleep." She found herself growing concerned. "How far away do the other two couples live?" she asked. It wasn't her place to say anything, but she thought that maybe on the road wasn't the best place for any of them to be right now.

"Not that far," he told her. He had a feeling he knew what she was thinking. "But Jenny and Adam have spare bedrooms. They can put them up for the night if necessary. They wouldn't want having anyone falling asleep at the wheel on their conscience," he told her. And then he added, "There's a spare room for us, as well."

His eyes met hers and she wasn't sure what he was thinking.

"Just wanted you to know," he added when she didn't say anything.

"I can drive us home if you're sleepy," Rachel volunteered. "Not 'us'," she corrected. "I mean you." And then she realized that that might present a problem in logistics since they had driven over in his car. "You might have to sleep over at my place, but that would just make you super early for your session with my dad and his physical therapy exercises," she said, trying to make him see the practical side of this and not think that she was trying to proposition him.

She looked at Wyatt and his expression gave nothing away.

It would have been nice if she were able to read him the way his friends seemed to be able to read one another, she thought.

Wyatt nodded as he rose to his feet. "That sounds like it has possibilities. I do like getting an early start, as does your father. First, though," he said, extending his hand to her to help her up, "we have to leave here."

Rachel grinned. "I do like your sense of organization."

"Oh, are you two going?" Jenny asked, rousing herself and sitting up straighter. She smiled, looking at Rachel. "I think I ate too much of your ziti. It's making me drowsy."

"Maybe it was the barbecue," Rachel suggested.

But Jenny shook her head at the suggestion. "Never the barbecue," she told her guest. Her voice dropped as she added, "Adam does his best, but, well…" Her voice trailed off as Jenny ended the statement with a well-meaning shrug.

Glancing around at the gathering, their hostess made a judgment call.

"Looks like the gang stays here tonight. I don't think they can see the road, much less be able to drive on it. You're welcome to stay here tonight, too," she offered, turning to look at Wyatt and Rachel.

"Thank you, but we both need to get an early start in the morning," Rachel told her. "Wyatt is still working on my dad's rehab, and as for me, I have got a restaurant to get ready."

Jenny began to walk the pair toward the front door. "I intend to come by to your restaurant sometime in the next couple of weeks, you know. You've definitely intrigued me."

"I'd love to see you there." Rachel looked around at the others who were in various stages of fading—mostly asleep. "Tell the others the same goes for them—and that I said goodbye."

Jenny nodded, but rather than agree, what she said was "Until the next time."

That sounded really nice, Rachel thought as she left with Wyatt.

Chapter Nineteen

"My father's going to be waiting up, so we're going to have to be really quiet when we come into the house. Are you capable of tiptoeing in?" she asked as she pulled Wyatt's car up to her front curb.

Rachel had driven back to her house under slight duress. Wyatt had protested that he wasn't really that sleepy and that he was perfectly capable of taking them to her home.

However, she wasn't buying it. Given the fact that he had consumed a couple glasses of wine within the last part of the barbecue, she had told him that there was no point in taking any unnecessary chances. And since she hadn't had any alcohol at all, that made her the perfect candidate to drive home.

"Does your father always wait up for you?" Wyatt asked as he got out of the passenger side.

The next second he found himself swallowing a curse. He had just hit his shin against the edge of the door because he wasn't used to getting out on the passenger side.

"Pretty much," Rachel admitted. "He got into the habit while he was convalescing at home after his heart attack," she told him. "Before that, he was always too busy, working at the restaurant. I suppose worrying about me gave him something to focus on."

Wyatt laughed softly to himself. "I guess you're not the only worrier in the family. Not that it's a bad thing," he quickly clarified, not wanting to set her off or offend her. "I do appreciate you worrying about me. What I mean by that is I appreciate you driving me home. Or rather to your house."

She shrugged. Rachel didn't view what she had done as a big deal. "I didn't think that reading about you being a fatality the next morning would be a perfect way to end this experience."

Wyatt nodded. "Can't argue with that," he told her, "although, for the record, I have driven home when I've been a lot sleepier than I am right now."

"Better safe than sorry," Rachel responded in a lowered voice.

Her fingers flew over the keypad as she quickly disarmed the security system and unlocked the front door. As she gestured for Wyatt to enter, she signaled for him to be quiet just in case he had forgotten.

Wyatt nodded, humoring her. It was obvious by his expression that he hadn't forgotten about not waking her father.

But the reminder turned out to be unnecessary. Rachel's father wasn't there.

Her father was not sitting in the recliner that had become his customary post while waiting for her. And a quick scan of the living room told her that he wasn't there, either.

"Maybe your father thought you'd get home safely since you were out with me and decided he could go to bed," Wyatt told her.

"Maybe," Rachel agreed but her tone let him know that she wasn't convinced. "But I'm still going to check on him."

Wyatt frowned slightly to himself. "You know, someday you're going to have to stop worrying. For your own good as well as his."

"I know," she answered, unfazed. "But someday isn't going to be tonight." She quickly hurried up the stairs.

Wyatt followed right behind her on the outside chance that something was wrong, although he felt pretty confident that it wasn't.

Arriving in front of her father's door, Rachel very quietly turned the doorknob and then peeked in. Wyatt was half a breath behind her.

Her father was lying in his bed, apparently sound asleep.

"Satisfied?" Wyatt whispered, withdrawing.

He was surprised that Rachel wasn't following right behind him and closing the door. Instead, she remained standing there, her eyes focused on her father.

She could feel Wyatt staring at her. "I just want to make sure he's breathing," she explained, taking a step closer into the bedroom.

She narrowed her eyes, focusing on her father's chest. Seeing it rise and fall evenly, she breathed a small sigh of relief.

And then, very slowly, she withdrew, closing the door behind her.

"Now are you satisfied?" Wyatt asked her, prepared to hear yet another objection.

"You probably think I'm being neurotic," Rachel guessed. She supposed she couldn't have really blamed him if he did. But he hadn't experienced what she had, she thought defensively. He hadn't found his parent lying on the floor after having a heart attack.

Besides, he and his mother had a more combative relationship. Wyatt probably didn't think in the same terms as she did.

"That's not exactly the word I'd use," Wyatt told her. "But I do think you're going to wind up making yourself crazy."

Because she cared what Wyatt thought, Rachel tried to make him understand her motivation. "I just didn't want to take a chance on something happening to my father while I was out having a good time," Rachel told him. "I wouldn't be able to forgive myself then."

"Rachel, you are a great daughter. A wonderful daughter," Wyatt corrected with feeling. "But that man—" he jerked his thumb toward her father's closed bedroom door "—is going to outlive you if you keep this up. You don't want to leave him alone, do you?"

Wyatt figured that, if anything, that might get to her enough to make her change a little.

"Well, if you put it that way..." Rachel's voice trailed off.

"I do," he answered assertively.

Rachel sighed. She supposed he had a point. "Okay, I'll try harder not to care."

"You can care all you want, Rachel. Just don't worry yourself into a frazzle," he told her. "I, for one, like you un-frazzled."

Somehow, standing there in the hallway like that, there suddenly hardly seemed to be any distance at all between them.

For one very sizzling moment, she thought Wyatt was going to kiss her. But then she was aware of his suddenly stepping back.

Taking a breath to steady his pulse, Wyatt told her, "If you point me toward where I'm supposed to sleep, I'll get out of your hair."

"Of course." She turned on her heel, walking down the hallway.

It was on the tip of her tongue to say that she didn't really mind having him in her hair, didn't really want him calling it an evening yet. But that would be tantamount to throwing herself at him. And what if he didn't feel like catching her? How would she recover from that?

How could she even face him after that?

No, it was better this way, keeping the lines from crossing, she counseled herself.

"There's another bedroom right here in the corner," she told him.

Reaching it, she opened the door, allowing him to look in. "It's kind of small," she apologized. "It used to be my mother's sewing room, but after she died, my father had someone come in and totally remodel it. It hurt him too much to look at it the way she had left it," she explained.

"Your father's a lucky man," Wyatt commented.

"How do you figure?" she asked, bewildered. She felt that losing the love of his life made her father the exact opposite of lucky.

He thought back to what she had told him about her parents. "To have had a love like that in his life even for a little while. There are men and women who go their entire lives and never experience anything that comes close to the kind of love your parents had. I guarantee that they would trade their souls to have that even for a little while."

She liked what Wyatt said, and she felt that he did have a point.

Rachel nodded. "When you put it that way, I guess my dad was lucky." But even so, a sadness swept over her. "It's just too bad he couldn't have been lucky for longer."

Wyatt looked at her for a long moment, his eyes saying things to her that he hadn't said out loud yet. "I guess you have to grab your happiness when you can. Whenever it shows up," he added, his voice growing even quieter.

It wasn't exactly clear which of them made

the first move, or if they just came together simultaneously in response to some inner, instinctive longing. But one moment it seemed that they were discussing her father and how lucky he had been to have found her mother the way he had, and the next moment they were in each other's arms, recreating the chemistry they had already managed to experience that very first time.

The moment their lips touched, the powerful explosion came. It meant that the first time hadn't just been a happy accident. What they had felt had been real.

Not only that, but it seemed to only get better, growing in intensity by the nanosecond.

His heart hammering hard, threatening to crack his rib cage, Wyatt drew back for a moment.

Rachel felt almost a frightening loss until she heard him saying, "If you want me to stop, you're going to have to tell me."

He didn't want the desire that was swelling within him to cause him to do something she really did not want.

Hearing Wyatt say that only excited her even more. He was being noble and putting her needs ahead of his own. She could feel every fiber of her body responding.

It was so close to his now, there wasn't even

room for so much as a whisper between them. Winding her arms around his neck, Rachel stood up on her toes and pressed herself against him.

"What makes you think I would even want you to," she asked in a husky voice.

The low, throaty sound excited Wyatt more than he could have ever imagined.

He gave himself in to the feeling.

His lips began to travel over the length of her, subtly arousing Rachel until she suddenly found herself way passed the point of no return.

Entwined, they fell against the bed that had yet to be christened.

Excitement swiftly rose to a hot, boiling point, reminding her body that it had been more than two whole, long years since she had experienced anything even remotely like this.

The next moment, encased in a fever pitch, she realized that she had *never* experienced anything even close to this. Without question, Elliott had never made her feel like this.

Wyatt made every inch of her body sing and ache as the desire she was experiencing continued to rise to overwhelming heights.

With swift, almost graceful movements, Wyatt removed her clothing, casting each garment aside and out of his way one at a time.

Once the clothing was gone, he was free to feast on her tempting, nude body.

With careful, precise movements, Wyatt was able to prime it to the point that she felt that any second now, she would wind up exploding all on her own.

He showed her no mercy.

Delighting in her body, Wyatt left a trail of hot, demanding kisses all along her quivering skin.

Rachel bit her lower lip to keep from moaning, absorbing every wonderful nuance that was vibrating over her damp body.

She couldn't just remain this passive receiver, a little voice in her head insisted. She needed to take an aggressive part in what was happening to her right at this moment.

With effort, she wove her fingers through Wyatt's remaining clothing, pulling the different pieces from his body until he was as naked as she was.

Her body was all but burning as she pressed her flesh against his, her tongue branding him, leaving a hot, moist trail along his chest and upper torso. She worked her way down along his body, going ever lower when she suddenly felt his hands on her shoulders.

In one smooth movement, Wyatt had switched

their positions. His body was looming over hers as he continued to forge and build on the initial trail that had been laid.

His lips brushed along her quivering navel, his tongue anointing her as his warm breath caressed her with a growing passion that all but made her cry out his name just as the first explosion hit, responding to the carefully placed flicks of his tongue at her most sensitive point.

The next moment his lips and tongue were recreating more explosions within her body, causing her to twist and moan in desperate longing as she used her body to cleave ever closer to him.

She felt Wyatt moving his way upward now, felt his breath on her face when he finally stopped and loomed over her.

Threading his fingers through hers, Wyatt looked into her eyes for one long moment before he began the final leg of their journey.

And then, entering her, Wyatt felt Rachel move her hips against his.

The dance began in earnest.

The initial pace was slow, growing more and more intense and urgent until they were suddenly racing up the summit, their ultimate goal the very peak of that mountain.

They were both desperate for the final release.

Desperate to experience that final, delicious explosion together, wrapped in each other's arms.

And then it happened, the exquisite finale that had them clinging to one another as if their very lives depended on it. They found themselves secretly praying that this wondrous sensation would never come to an end.

And then, panting, spent, their hearts hammering in what felt like an almost rhythmic echo of one another, they were encased in a euphoria that was nothing short of fantastic.

A euphoria that slowly faded into the ether even while it was still simultaneously vibrating and humming all through their bodies.

Spent, Wyatt sighed contentedly.

Rolling off her, he gathered Rachel into his arms and held her against him, savoring what had just transpired between them.

He waited for his heart to stop pounding so hard, and when he could finally catch his breath, he pressed a kiss against her forehead.

He couldn't even begin to put into words just how good that felt.

"Well, I didn't see that coming," he whispered, his breath curling around her cheek.

"That," Rachel admitted, "makes two of us."

She drew herself up on her elbow for a moment, her eyes shining. "I love surprises. Don't you?"

"I do now," he admitted. As his breathing began to level off, he stroked her hair, thinking how very lucky he was to have found her.

If he hadn't asked her out…

But he had, he thought, and now he was the richer for it.

It was his turn to prop himself up on his elbow and look down into her face. Was it his imagination, or did she just grow more beautiful every time he looked at her?

His heart swelled. He had never felt happier, and from where he was, it promised only to get better.

A wicked smile curved his lips. "Would you like to go again?" he asked seductively.

Wyatt felt her laugh against him, her delight spreading a warm, infectious web all around him.

"I thought you'd never ask," she said, surrendering herself to the feeling and to Wyatt.

The night only grew better from there.

Chapter Twenty

It was an amazing six weeks, each day filled to capacity from beginning to end. The days seemed to be filled with easy laughter, and the nights—with lovemaking that raised her happiness to astonishing, breathtaking levels—made her eagerly look forward to the next.

Rachel didn't know that she could feel this wonderful for this long.

It seemed as if she was virtually walking on air. Or at the very least, five inches off the ground.

Not only that, but she found herself wanting to sing—all the time.

Heaven knew it had never been nearly this

wonderful when she had fallen for Elliott. Although she had thought that had been her first experience with love, what she had felt was not even remotely close to what was happening to her now.

She also discovered that she didn't get nearly as tired any more. She slept in small snatches and felt refreshed enough when she woke up to be able to go on. Rachel even managed to catch up with her online classes without her face suddenly communing with her keyboard.

There was no way to predict how long this euphoric state was going to last. After all, all good things had to come to an end and this definitely came under the heading of a "good thing."

A *very good thing*, Rachel amended as she moved around the yet unopened restaurant, cheerfully taking care of all the last-minute details needed in order to achieve a good day.

When their paths crossed, Johanna was so taken with the incredibly cheerful young woman that she stopped walking.

"Well, you certainly seem like you're sitting on top of the world," Johanna commented. "Does it have anything to do with a certain blond, broad-shouldered hunk—or am I not supposed to ask? I wouldn't want to get my head bitten off, especially not less than two months before the holidays. I just got a new dress for Christmas and it really would look a little strange if I was headless."

A wide smile curved Rachel's mouth. "Just so you know, I've given up biting off heads for the foreseeable future."

"So this new delightful version of you *is* due to the hunky Wyatt Watson?" Johanna asked, aware that there was a time not all that long ago that she would have been pushing the limit of Rachel's patience.

To her surprise, the assistant manager heard Rachel actually admit, "Yes, it is."

Rather than say anything, a delighted Johanna threw her arms around the young woman she had known for most of the latter's life.

"I cannot tell you how happy that makes me." She lowered her voice slightly to say, "That Elliott character just wasn't worth any of your precious time. I am ever so thrilled that this young man came along when he did—for both your father's sake *and for yours*."

Rachel's eyes crinkled as she laughed. "I kind of gathered that."

"Okay—" Johanna looked into Rachel's eyes "—so what's next?"

"I'm just planning on enjoying this one step at a time, Johanna," Rachel told her.

Johanna looked rather surprised. "And that's it?"

"That's it," Rachel echoed. "I learned my lesson the last time. Making plans is highly overrated. Just because you make them doesn't mean they're going to stick, and I now know that those plans can very easily just fall through."

Johanna nodded. "Yes—if you're making those plans involving a rat or a snake. Not a fairy-tale prince," the woman said with a dreamy expression on her face.

"Don't get carried away, Johanna," Rachel warned as she pulled out yet another inventory list to go over when she got the chance today.

"I'm not—although I'd say that your father has that department covered," Johanna confessed, her words managing to thoroughly confuse Rachel.

Rachel folded the list in half, putting it temporarily in her back pocket as she stared at Johanna. "Come again?"

A mysterious smile descended on the woman's expressive face. Drawing a little closer, Johanna dropped her voice as she asked, "Can you keep a secret?"

Rachel's answer was an honest one. "If I have to," she responded.

Johanna drew even closer to the young woman. For a second, it seemed as if she was going to whisper into Rachel's ear. But rather than say anything at all, Johanna held up her left hand for Rachel's perusal.

It took Rachel several seconds to realize that her father's friend and main confidante for so many years was displaying a small, tasteful diamond ring worn on the appropriate finger.

Rachel's eyes grew huge. It was all she could do to keep back a gasp. "You and my father?" she asked incredulously.

"Well, it wasn't Rumpelstiltskin," Johanna told her with a laugh.

Rachel could hardly believe that it had finally happened. She had been hoping that the two people she cared about would get together for years now. Admittedly, Rachel had been aware that her father and Johanna cared for one another for a very long time, but she had given up thinking that anything would come of it.

Tears rose to her eyes, threatening to spill out as she threw her arms around the woman. "I think this is just wonderful!" she cried, delighted. "Why didn't you say anything?"

"I thought I should leave that to your father, but you know what he's like with communication. If he can't yell or grumble, it usually goes unsaid," Johanna confided.

Rachel rolled her eyes. "Don't I know it. Well, I am beyond thrilled and you're perfect for him.

You're the only one who can put up with him without giving in to the urge to strangle the man."

Johanna winked. "Want to know a secret? I've learned how to contain my emotions," she confided with a laugh. "And your father's a very good man. He's worth a few antacid tablets I've had to swallow."

And then, just as suddenly, the sparkle vanished from Johanna's eyes as she stared over Rachel's shoulder. The expression that came over her face sent a chill down Rachel's spine.

"Johanna, what's wrong?" Rachel heard herself asking, almost afraid of the answer.

When the woman didn't say anything, Rachel turned around to see just what it was that had changed her expression like that.

When she saw what—or who—it was, her heart all but stopped.

Why?

The question echoed in her mind as she saw the man who was walking toward her.

"Hello, Rachel. You're even more beautiful than I remember."

Elliott.

What was he doing here?

Why was he here?

Rachel heard the words and couldn't believe

that Elliott was actually saying them to her—or had the nerve to say them at all.

She saw Johanna fade back. For better or worse, the woman was letting her handle this on her own.

Rachel squared her shoulders. "What are you doing here, Elliott?" Her voice was cold, distant.

"Penance, atonement," he told her, slowly drawing a little closer. "Anything you want to call it." His eyes were searching her face for a trace of compassion. "I was wrong to leave like that when I did. You needed me and I wasn't there for you. You don't know how much I regret that."

If Elliott was trying to make amends, it was much too late for that. She wasn't the young woman she had once been and she wasn't easily taken in by words she knew were empty.

"And it took you two years to come to that conclusion?" she asked.

"No," he told her. "Two years to work up my nerve to apologize."

He had always been the impetuous type, given to acting on impulse. That explained why he had fallen for and married Dora the way he had.

"Does your wife know you're here, apologizing like this?" she asked. In her opinion, he was being despicable.

"I've left her," he said. His voice grew emotional as he went on to tell her, "I made a mistake, Rachel.

I realize that now." Elliott stepped closer, attempting to take her hand in his but she pulled back. As much as she had once welcomed it, the thought of him touching her now was almost unbearable.

In one fell swoop the man was actually dumping his wife and his baby. What in heaven's name had she ever seen in him? How could she have been so blind?

"And the baby?" Rachel asked pointedly.

"Dora will get custody, of course." He tried again, stepping closer to her. "Look, I'll admit it. I made a lot of mistakes."

"That's a flesh-and-blood baby you're trying to abandon, Elliott. She's not a 'mistake,'" Rachel told him coldly.

"You're right," he freely conceded, sounding as if he was willing to say anything to get her to let him back into her life. "You've always been right. Look, Rachel, I just really want us to have a fresh start."

"Well, you can certainly have a fresh start," Rachel told him without reservation. But the next moment, as he happily began to move toward her, she added, "But there is no 'us.'"

Elliott looked at her in disbelief. "You want me to leave?"

"I want you to go where I never have to see

you again," she told him, "so yes. Go." It was an order now, not a request.

It was a request he wasn't allowing to sink in. He shook his head. "You don't mean that."

The man was insufferable. Again she couldn't believe that she had been so impervious to all his faults and shortcomings. Had it been that important to her to have someone love her?

She blocked the thought from her mind.

"Oh, but I never meant anything more in my life," Rachel told him.

Elliott's face darkened. "You're going to be sorry you said that."

"What I am sorry about is that I didn't say it to you earlier and I wound up wasting three years of my life, thinking we were going to get married," she told him. "I'm with a wonderful man now—"

"Oh, I get it." There was a cruelty in his voice as he regarded her. "And you think you're going to get him to marry you," Elliott said with a sneer.

"I am not going to get him to do anything. I don't play games," she informed him. "But I do know that five minutes with him is worth more than those three years I spent with you."

There was anger in her eyes as she asked him, "Now, are you going, or do I have to have Eduardo throw you out?" referring to the security guard who doubled as a bouncer.

"I'd listen to her if I were you," Wyatt said, coming up behind Rachel. He placed his hands on her shoulders in a gesture that could only be construed as protective. "Because I'm guessing that you probably already know that Rachel always means whatever she says."

Elliott's eyes narrowed as he shot Wyatt a hostile glare, looking him up and down. His mouth registered disdain and disapproval. "I take it that you're the new guy."

"No," Wyatt contradicted. "I'm not the *new* guy. I'm the permanent guy." He took a step toward the former boyfriend, who looked as if he had grown paunchy in the two years that had gone by. "Rachel's not going to tell you again, but I will. Go while you still can."

A look akin to fear passed over Elliott's features. He scowled at Rachel. "You'll be sorry," he predicted again.

"Not for even one minute," she answered, slipping her hand into Wyatt's.

The gesture presented a united front.

Like a rat leaving a sinking ship, Elliott left quickly, muttering under his breath.

"So that's the ex, huh?" Wyatt asked after Elliott had cleared out. "I thought you had better taste in men."

"I do—now," she told him. "I was young and very naive when I was in high school. And Elliott was on the football team."

Wyatt laughed, slipping his arm around her shoulders and pulling her against him. "I guess everyone's entitled to one mistake."

"Is the snake gone?" Johanna asked, emerging out of the small office where she had disappeared, presumably to allow Rachel to deal with her ex on her own.

"He slithered underground," Rachel told her.

"What did he want?" Johanna asked innocently.

"Rachel here, apparently," Wyatt answered.

They weren't fooling her. Rachel had a feeling that Johanna had only disappeared in order to call Wyatt, allowing him to come and rescue her if need be.

"Interesting how you just happened to appear out of nowhere," Rachel commented, looking at Wyatt.

He grinned, still maintaining innocence. "I'm lucky like that," he answered. He refrained from saying anything about the fact that Johanna had texted him the moment that Elliott had made his appearance at the restaurant. Wyatt had dropped everything to get there.

Rachel looked at him with the same wide-eyed innocence she had just been subjected to. "Are you here for a reason?"

"Do I need one?" he asked.

"No," she answered honestly. "But you don't normally pop up in the middle of the morning, that's all. I just thought I'd ask."

"Well," Wyatt said, taking her hand and leading her off to where the desserts had been placed on ice just before they were stored for sale. "As it happens, I *am* here for a reason."

Rachel looked up at him, wondering if she should be bracing herself. She no longer believed that she could continue to live in a dream world and that everything was going to resolve itself to her satisfaction. She knew that when she expected the best was when she became an easy target for disappointment.

"All right," Rachel said, wanting to get this over with. "You might as well tell me what it is."

"You sound as if you're waiting for the judge to read you your death sentence," he told her.

Rachel didn't see a reason to lie. "That all depends on what you have to tell me."

He had come prepared, but this was turning

out to be harder than he had anticipated. He had never done this before.

"Let me start out by saying that I have had a wonderful two months," Wyatt told her. "When I took this assignment, I never thought things would wind up turning out this way."

He was going too slowly and it was killing her.

"But…?" she said when he paused. Rachel felt as if she was dying inside. Part of her wanted to put off what he was going to say for as long as she could because she was certain this was the beginning of the end. The other part wanted to face up to what she felt was the disappointment that was waiting to take the air out of her balloons as she sailed over the Grand Canyon.

"But it's time for me to tell you what I'm feeling," Wyatt continued.

She felt a chill slide down between her shoulders that was really hard to ignore. "And that is?" she asked in a whisper.

He took a breath, then finally said, "I love you, Rachel."

She blinked. She had hoped, but hadn't expected. Hearing the words was thrilling. "You what?" she cried, stunned.

"Love you," he repeated. "You have heard of love, right?"

Her heart slammed against her chest. "Yes, oh yes," she said breathlessly.

He needed an answer to his question. "So what I want to know is—"

"Yes," Rachel cried, before he had the chance to finish.

"Yes?" Wyatt asked uncertainly.

"Yes," she repeated with emphasis.

"To?" he asked, not clear just what she was saying yes to.

"To what I hope is the question you're asking," Rachel told him.

Okay, he needed to make this as clear as he could. "I'm asking you to marry me because I've never felt this way before and don't think I ever will again. I know a once-in-a-lifetime thing when I come across it and—"

The grin all but split her face. "I've already given you my answer, Wyatt, so if you know what's good for you," she told him, "you'll stop talking and kiss me."

He laughed then. "Yes, ma'am, happy to accommod—"

Wyatt didn't get to finish the sentence because her lips were already sealed to his.

Sealed in happiness and in utter, complete, zealous passion.

Epilogue

"Well, ladies, clear your calendars for the last Saturday of the month. It looks like our track record still stands," Maizie announced happily the moment Theresa and Cilia walked into her family room.

"You mean—" Cilia began, only to be cut off by Theresa.

"Yes, she does," Wyatt's "aunt" declared. Smiling broadly, she placed her wedding invitation on the table. "I got this in the mail this morning."

Maizie produced her own invitation and put it right beside the first one. "George hand-delivered mine last night." She looked at her friends with no small sense of triumph. "It's written out to all three of us," she told the other two women.

"Well, then I won't say anything about being the low woman on the totem pole," Cilia said, since she hadn't personally received hers.

"Cilia, a victory for one of us is a victory for all of us," Maizie reminded her friend.

"I know, I know," Cilia assured her. Turning toward Theresa, she said, "Your cousin must be ecstatic."

The latter smiled broadly. "For once, Ariel is speechless—something else Wyatt is grateful for," she added with a wink.

Utterly delighted about this latest wedding they were instrumental in bringing about, the three lifelong friends began to eagerly talk among themselves, making plans for that day.

George Fenelli knocked on the door behind which, for forty-five years, brides had been getting dressed and preparing to take vows that would unite them with the men who had won their hearts.

"Come on in, Dad," Rachel said, knowing it had to be her father, since Johanna was here with her, fussing with her veil.

George walked in, his heart swelling almost before the moment he took in the sight of his daughter wearing the floor-length wedding gown that his wife had worn all those years ago.

When she had told him that Wyatt had proposed, George had offered to buy Rachel her own, new wedding gown, but she wouldn't hear of it. She said that she wanted to wear her mother's. He couldn't find the words to tell her how happy that made him.

He didn't have to.

"Well?" Rachel asked, turning around to face her father as she smoothed down the bridal gown while Johanna carefully adjusted her veil so it wouldn't get caught.

"You look absolutely beautiful," he whispered, his voice growing hoarse from the tears that were gathering in his throat. "I just really wish your mother was here to see this."

"She is," Johanna assured both of them.

Another knock was heard as a very pregnant Myra peered into the room. "It's time, Rachel."

They all knew what that meant.

"I'd better get out with the others," Johanna told Rachel. "See you up front," she added, giving her new stepdaughter's hand a squeeze before she left the room.

"Ready, honey?" George asked.

"More than ready," she answered as her father handed her the wedding bouquet. Strains of the wedding march were beginning to fill the room.

George slipped his arm through Rachel's. "Then let's get this show on the road."

"Let's," Rachel agreed.

It was hard for Rachel to walk so slowly at her father's side when what she really wanted to do was race up the aisle to Wyatt so she could hear the words that would forever bind the two of them together.

The moment she walked into the church proper at her father's side, her eyes immediately found Wyatt's. His smile instantly sank into her soul, drawing her to him. Rachel honestly didn't remember walking from one end of the church to the other, she just remembered reaching her long-awaited destination.

"You came," Wyatt whispered, repeating words he had said to her on their very first date.

"Wouldn't miss it for the world," she said, echoing her reply.

They turned in unison to face the priest, both more than ready to begin their new life.

Together.

* * * * *

Don't miss previous romances
by Marie Ferrarella, from
Harlequin Special Edition:

Secrets of Forever
Coming to a Crossroads
Her Right-Hand Cowboy
Bridesmaid for Hire
The Lawman's Romance Lesson
Adding Up to Family

COMING NEXT MONTH FROM

HARLEQUIN

SPECIAL EDITION

#2863 A RANCHER'S TOUCH
Return to the Double C • by Allison Leigh

Rosalind Pastore is starting over: new town, new career, new lease on life. And when she buys a dog grooming business, she gets a new neighbor in gruff rancher Trace Powell. Does giving in to their feelings mean a chance to heal...or will Ros's old life come back to haunt her?

#2864 GRAND-PRIZE COWBOY
Montana Mavericks: The Real Cowboys of Bronco Heights
by Heatherly Bell

Rancher Boone Dalton has felt like an outsider in Bronco Heights ever since his family moved to town. When a prank lands him a makeover with Sofia Sanchez, he's determined to say "Hell no!" Sofia is planning a life beyond Bronco Heights, and she's not looking for a forever cowboy. But what if her heart is telling her Boone might just be The One?

#2865 HER CHRISTMAS FUTURE
The Parent Portal • by Tara Taylor Quinn

Dr. Olivia Wainwright is the accomplished neonatologist she is today because she never wants another parent to feel the loss that she did. Her marriage never recovered, but one night with her ex-husband, Martin, leaves her fighting to save a pregnancy she never thought possible. Can Olivia and Martin heal the past and find family with this unexpected Christmas blessing?

#2866 THE LIGHTS ON KNOCKBRIDGE LANE
Garnet Run • by Roan Parrish

Raising a family was always Adam Mills' dream, although solo parenting and moving back to tiny Garnet Run certainly were not. Adam is doing his best to give his daughter the life she deserves—including accepting help from their new, reclusive neighbor Wes Mobray to fulfill her Christmas wish...

#2867 A CHILD'S CHRISTMAS WISH
Home to Oak Hollow • by Makenna Lee

Eric McKnight's only priority is his disabled daughter's happiness. Her temporary nanny, Jenny Winslet, is eager to help make Lilly's Christmas wishes come true. She'll even teach grinchy Eric how to do the season right! It isn't long before visions of family dance in Eric's head. But when Jenny leaves them for New York City... there's still one Christmas wish he has yet to fulfill.

#2868 RECIPE FOR A HOMECOMING
The Stirling Ranch • by Sabrina York

To heal from her abusive marriage, Veronica James returns to her grandmother's bookshop. But she has to steel her heart against the charms of her first love, rancher Mark Stirling. He's never stopped longing for a second chance with the girl who got away—but when their "friends with benefits" deal reveals emotions that run deep, Mark is determined to convince Veronica that they're the perfect blend.

YOU CAN FIND MORE INFORMATION ON UPCOMING HARLEQUIN TITLES, FREE EXCERPTS AND MORE AT HARLEQUIN.COM.

HSECNM0921